SLEEPING WOLF

A WATERWAY CHRONICLE ADVENTURE

BOOK 3

BY MATTHEW GORE

Sleeping Wolf, A Waterway Chronicle Adventure
Book 3

Paperback ISBN: 979-8-9911138-3-0

Cover Design: Thom Hoyman

Dedication

This book is dedicated to:

My dear friends, Yvonne and Randy. You two are more responsible than anyone for continually stoking the fires of my nautical obsession, spanning more than three decades. We've cruised together, explored together, and looked at boats together in ports and harbors all over North America. No matter what trip, trouble, or waterway mischief we could cook up, your response was as constant as gravity: "We're in!"

You've been the older brother and sister we've needed so many times in this crazy and blessed life. We treasure you both, and I am grateful for all your encouragement and support as I navigate my way to becoming a better storyteller.

YT & RT . . . Thank you both, we love you.

Chapter 1

Germany, September 1944

Rear Admiral Ernst Weidlinger stared thoughtfully at the tabletop chart that filled much of the secret briefing room. The forgotten ten-by-ten space lay tucked away in a dark corner of the lower basement beneath the German naval installation known as the *Wolfsschanze*, or "Wolf's Lair," in East Prussia. The immense nautical chart the men quietly considered encompassed the entire Atlantic Ocean and the eastern half of the United States, including the Mississippi River and the Gulf of Mexico. Low hanging cigarette smoke combined with the bright overhead lights obscured the faces of the Rear Admiral and the only other man in the room, Commodore Dieter Kessler. The two men had been pivotal in every aspect of German submarine warfare for decades. On December 7, 1941, the same day that Japan attacked Pearl Harbor, Adolf Hitler had given approval for "Operation Drumbeat." The ambitious naval mission sent German U-boats into the Atlantic and Gulf of Mexico with devastating effects against the US and all Allied forces. As Admiral Karl Donitz commanded the fleet of deadly submarines surging across the Atlantic, the first half of 1942 earned the nickname "American Shooting Season," as the German Wolf Pack sank more than one hundred vessels in the first three months of the secret operation. German military brass praised Admiral Donitz for the operation's success, but Weidlinger and Kessler had always been in the shadows, developing and perfecting the Donitz's deadly gray predators.

But now, two years later, things had changed. For the last twelve months, German forces experienced a decisive turn of the tide as the losses of battle after battle continued to compound. If something did not change soon, Germany would face certain defeat. The Führer himself dispatched a defiant directive to the command of every branch of the German military, ordering them to create a strategy to stem this tide of loss.

Weidlinger and Kessler were building a new fleet of

Mark XXI submarines as quickly as they could. The radical new design was the most advanced submarine ever conceived, much less built. The new boats could run faster and stay submerged much longer than any other submarine. If the German Navy could get enough of the advanced subs into the Atlantic, it would change the face of the war. But both men knew that despite their efforts, the deadly new war machines were probably too little, too late. The scales of the war had tipped so far that the duo's next generation of lethal gray wolves would likely not reach the battlefield in time. But Weidlinger and Kessler had one last card to play.

Both German officers were in their fifties. Weidlinger was a thick tree stump of a man that liked the finer things in life. His graying temples topped healthy, reddened jowls that always accepted a second helping and one more glass of red wine. His partner stood in stark contrast. Kessler was a walking skeleton. The bones of his thin face stood out against the stretched skin, and his cold blue eyes wore dark circles that were constant. He was calculating and fastidious. His immaculately fitted uniform was spotless and never creased. The six-foot-one officer could stand ready for an inspection by the Führer himself, any time of the day or night.

"What was your last communication with Commander Schreiber?" Weidlinger asked.

After exhaling a breath of cigarette smoke, adding to the

grittiness of the room, Kessler answered. "He reports all systems are functioning and that all pressure tests have far exceeded design specifications."

"Good. And the weapons systems?"

"Repeated test firings of the deck-mounted rockets have been flawless after surfacing. The new formulations of paints and seawater seals have also outperformed design objectives."

Weidlinger nodded with approval.

The one and only X-601 was smaller and even more advanced than the XXI boats. The highly secret one-off design was the pet project of the two German submariners, and only a handful of people within the German Navy even knew it existed. Subs used by the US Navy ran at speeds between eight and ten knots while submerged. The X-601 could run twenty knots while submerged. Its retractable snorkel made it possible for the deadly wolf to remain submerged or even sit lurking on a shallow bottom for up to thirty days without surfacing. The X-601 had eight torpedoes and could fire six modified high-yield V-2 rockets from its newly designed deck launching mounts. These more advanced V-2's each had a range of two hundred fifty miles.

Kessler pointed to a location three hundred miles off the east coast of Florida. "Captain Schreiber will take the 601 submerged from here, all the way into the Gulf of Mexico and to the entrance of the Mississippi River. If he has remained undetected, he will proceed directly up the river as far as Baton Rouge. There, he will fire his new rockets northeast and northwest, directly into the heartland of the United States. Not since their civil war has the US witnessed war and destruction within their mainland. This will strike fear and doubt into the American forces, pulling them back to defend their home."

"And if they detect him?" Weidlinger asked.

"Then Captain Schreiber will initiate the Sleeping Wolf Protocol and purposely ground the boat on the bottom in silence. The new coating formulations and air lock seals enable the 601 to remain submerged . . . indefinitely, theoretically. The new air lock docking hatch design will allow another sub to dock with the 601, resupplying her to continue the mission months or even years later," Kessler said.

Weidlinger's slow head nod acknowledged the grizzly detail of the mission. He knew the 601 could sleep on the bottom indefinitely, but the crew's lives would become a draining hourglass the minute the protocol was engaged, in a countdown to the end of food and oxygen. "And his crew is aware of this protocol?"

"The captain hand selected each member of the crew with this contingency of the mission in mind. They are all prepared to serve our nation to the greatest potential effect, no matter the cost," Kessler said.

Weidlinger stared silently at the large chart. "It is a brilliant plan, but most likely a suicide mission."

"At this stage of the war, aren't they all?"

Weidlinger nodded. " I suppose so," he said before exhaling another plume of smoky fog down across the chart.

"If the 601 cannot penetrate the mainland and rain terror upon the Americans, Captain Schreiber and his crew will die with honor and set the stage for the Fourth Reich to be born and rise from the ashes of our defeat. He will sail east tomorrow at dawn," Kessler said.

"Did my specially requested provisions make it in time?" Weidlinger asked.

For the first time during the somber meeting, there was a reason for Kessler to smile. "Yes, Admiral. I had twenty cases of the finest meats, cheeses, and wine delivered and stowed aboard yesterday."

"And the final provisions?"

"One coded lockbox with one unit for each member of the crew," replied Kessler.

Weidlinger's smile faded, replaced by a thoughtful gaze. "With either outcome of this glorious mission, Captain Schreiber and his crew will become the most remembered and celebrated heroes our nation has ever known."

The trip across the Atlantic passed in record time. The submerged speed of the X-601 was impressive, and the boat performed perfectly. Two hundred miles northwest of the lower Florida Keys, the stealthy sub surfaced for only the second time since leaving port. The newly designed hatch on the top of the sail hissed as it opened. It was just after midnight, and the half-moon combined with scattered clouds concealed the low riding profile of the sub well within the small waves. The moonlight that filtered through the clouds created patches of sparkles on the dark, warm autumn waters near the Keys. Captain Schreiber and his first officer, Otto Becker, emerged from the hatch and each man took their first breaths of fresh air in more than a week. Otto stretched his arms high, enjoying the brief respite of not having a short ceiling filled with pipes and cables ever present just overhead. Schreiber scanned the area with binoculars for any signs of surface traffic. He and his deadly X-601 were alone, and quietly making four knots across a light chop during this last brief pause before heading into the breach.

"I will miss this the most," Schreiber said, looking out across the sparkling dark sea as his boat's bow sliced through the water like a menacing shark.

"The calm before the storm of battle, Captain?"

"No. The thrum of the deck under my boots. A good ship and a good crew. And the smell of the sea and mist against my cheeks." The captain took a deep breath of the salty night air.

Otto wisely picked up the significance of the moment and, without a word, mirrored his captain's actions.

"In teams of four, give each man five minutes up here before we dive," Schreiber said.

"Yes, Captain. Right away." After a brief pause, Otto said, "Captain, we have the finest ship ever conceived, manned by the finest crew in the German Navy. We will be victorious in our mission."

"Yes, Otto, we will. One way or another . . . we will be victorious."

Twenty-four hours later and one hundred forty kilometers from the outer entrance of the Mississippi River, the X-601 was reeling in the boat's air snorkel from a submerged depth of ten meters when an excited call came from the sonarman.

"Captain, a large American patrol boat, six hundred meters off our starboard quarter. They were sitting idle, so we did not detect them. Their sonar is now active and they are on a course directly toward us."

"Did you send the encoded message with our position to naval command?"

"I did, Captain."

Calmly, the captain released the internal radio mic from its latch and keyed the mic.

"Alarm. I repeat, alarm," he said, before replacing the mic. Schreiber looked to his oberbootsmann stationed behind the helmsmen and, remaining eerily calm, gave his next command. "Chief of the Boat, make your depth sixty meters."

"Making our depth sixty meters, aye, Captain."

Schreiber nodded. "Maintain speed and bring us to around to three hundred ten degrees."

"Aye, changing course to three-one-zero degrees," came the echoed command. The sub creaked and groaned, like the world's largest oil drum being twisted by a pair of enormous hands, as the water drag of the sharp course correction stressed the steel hull of the boat. Six tense minutes passed as Captain Schreiber stared straight ahead, listening and concentrating. His objective was so close. Another few hours and he could have quietly steered his boat into the mouth of the river, evading the active search area of the US subchasers. But now, the battle-worn captain's muscles tightened as the grim reality of the Sleeping Wolf Protocol rose from a possibility . . . to most likely. Schreiber's stone-faced stare and lined features revealed nothing. His cold and calculated expression never changed, as the next call from the sonarman came from over his shoulder.

"Captain, I have another contact approaching from the west. Eight hundred meters and closing fast."

Before the sonarman's report was complete, the faint pings of the American ships' sonar began echoing throughout the interior of the X-601.

"All Stop," called the captain. "Rig for quiet."

X-601's primary engine wound down, and an eerie silence settled throughout the boat. Red lights, signaling the boat's "battle stations" status, painted the sub's interior in small crimson pools that reflected off the faces of the German submariners. Defiant young sailors stood frozen at their stations, staring upward with an ear keenly trained above, listening for the sounds of the approaching hounds as they churned the surface, hungry for prey. The first distant explosion reverberated through the hull, replacing the sailor's anxious looks with solemn faces of resignation.

"SHY-suh," Otto whispered.

The next three explosions came even closer to the sub, shaking the entire boat and blinking the interior red lights with each recurring shockwave.

"Flood forward ballast tanks slowly and increase our depth to eighty meters," the captain whispered.

Seconds later, two additional explosions shook and rattled the sub to its frames, causing groans and strains in the boat that even the most seasoned submariner hoped they'd never hear.

"XO, you have the conn," Schreiber said to his first officer, who seemed puzzled that the captain would leave the bridge at such a critical moment.

"Aye, Captain," Otto replied in a somber voice.

Schreiber quickly made his way to his tight-quartered cabin and closed the door behind him. He reached and removed a small oil painting of a waterfront village, maybe on the Black Sea, that he'd mounted directly above his tiny desk on the bulkhead. Schreiber depressed a spot in the center of the bulkhead where the painting had hung, and a hidden compartment opened with a click, revealing a small safe door and combination dial. The captain quickly dialed the combination from memory and opened the door. The interior of the safe held a single manilla folder. Schreiber stared in at the folder for a few long seconds. He knew this was always a potential, maybe even the likely outcome, of this mission. But he was still oddly shocked that this moment might actually be happening. Reaching into the safe, Schreiber removed the folder into the light of his cabin. Printed across the front of the folder, in bold letters was *Streng Geheim: Schlafender Wolf Protokoll*. (Top Secret: Sleeping Wolf Protocol.)

Eighty meters above, on the surface, Walt Simpson, the forty-one-year-old captain of the US subchaser SC-412, had just given the order to increase the depth setting for the next barrage of charges and make another circle around their current position.

"They're here," Simpson said to his XO Joe Hallsey. "I can feel it. We'll drop another round on them and see what we can catch."

"I don't like how close he's gotten to the mouth of the river," Hallsey replied. "We need to break his back, right here."

The surface explosions from the next barrage of depth charges shook the entire ship as it sent plumes of white water into the air on this dark night just off the coast of Louisiana.

"That's exactly what I aim to do, Joe."

Chapter 2

Stock Island, in the Florida Keys, 2022

My clean, but well-worn cargo shorts and Water Horse Expeditions T-shirt felt good this morning. The sunshine and salt air had been good medicine these last eight weeks. I actually had something resembling a tan. My morning walks around the decks of our one-hundred-forty-foot home and research vessel for hire helped keep my mind busy and off more troubling things. But on this morning's rounds, I'd only run into one of the five crew members aboard after two bow-to-stern passes on deck. I met our first officer, Jerry Styles, as he stepped out of a midship hatch.

"Where is everybody?" I asked.

"Rudy's got Beau and Jas lending a hand in the engine room this morning," Jerry answered.

I almost spit out a sip of coffee. "Rudy asked for help?"

"Well, I think he kinda volun-told them this morning, after he made what he called 'one-armed super-omelets' for everyone."

"That sounds about right." I laughed.

Rudy Giles was our chief engineer, and his years at sea made him our resident old salt and uncle-type to the Water Horse team. He was still recovering from an injury he'd suffered on our last assignment. And although his arm was still in a sling, it didn't seem to affect his ability or speed in his duties. However, the reality that a few jobs in the engine room required at least two hands would reluctantly force Rudy to ask for help for a few more weeks.

I made my way down the brightly lit steps and into the engine room compartment to check on their progress. Once inside the holy place of the boat, I walked over to the back starboard corner of the compartment where the piping and pumps of *Water Horse*'s large water filtration system lived. Rudy stood, a mug in his good hand, looking down at two sets of legs protruding from beneath the collection of pipes and pumps. The owner of each pair of legs was easy to identify. One pair was big, hairy, scarred, and scratched. That would be our former marine and deck boss, Beau Benson. I liked Beau, but his legs weren't much to look at. The other set, however, was long, muscled, smooth, and beautifully tan. Those belonged to Jas. She was our technology wrangler aboard. A former world-champion free diver, Jas's prowess as a world-class athlete was matched only by her proficiency with our camera systems, drones, and ROVs we used in our work with visiting research clients. If I held my mug up to block 50 percent of the picture, it wasn't a bad view to start the morning.

"I can't get the wrench in the right angle on that bolt on the back side," Beau grunted and strained.

Rudy looked at me and rolled his eyes. "Turn your wrench over, Marine."

"How can turning the wrench over . . . oh, never mind, got it. Jas, can you pull that bolt out now?"

"Got it," Jas said.

Our newest crew member, Harper, an eighty-pound Scottish deer hound, sat next to Rudy in his usual assistant supervisor role. On our last assignment, we'd found Harper and a fisherman adrift, starving and suffering from exposure in a small open boat in the middle of the Gulf. Unfortunately, the fisherman passed away, too weak to recover. But Rudy nursed the gray hairy beast back to health and now the two were inseparable. Rudy named him Harper after an old friend, and now he was a valuable part of the Water Horse team. Harper left his post next to Rudy long enough for me to apply a good behind the ear scratch.

"How we doing this morning, gang?" I asked.

"Morning, Captain," Beau grunted from beneath the machinery.

"Looks like the price of a Rudy-Super-Omelet has gone up," I said.

"Brotha! Preach!" Beau's voice rang from the confined space.

"Rudy, they're always worth it," Jas called out.

"I may turn you both into wrench monkeys yet," Rudy said. "These filters will need changing again before you know it. Just wait till you taste my Two-Armed-Super-Omelet."

"When's that sling coming off again?" Beau asked over the clinks of wrench turns.

Jas kicked sideways with her running sneaker and caught Beau in the shin.

"Oww," Beau grunted. "I was just kidding."

"Just keep turning that bolt, jarhead," Jas barked.

Rudy and I both laughed. Minutes later, with the new filters in place, Beau and Jas shimmied out from beneath the pipes and valves and stood. The confined space left Jas standing a little closer to me than normal.

"Morning, Michael," she said, without any effort to widen the space between us.

"Morning," I replied. I reached and picked up a shop rag on the nearby bench. "You've got a little . . ." as I wiped a black smudge off her cheek.

"Oh, thanks," she said, smiling.

Without a word, Rudy and Beau slinked off toward the engine room entrance hatch. These moments between Jas and me had become more and more frequent in the last few months, but neither of us knew exactly what it was. I think the crew had more awareness of it than we did on most days.

"Any news from Morgan?" she asked.

"Two days ago he sent a text telling me that that meeting with his Naval Intelligence buddy finally got put on the books. I'm going to take the call this afternoon."

"Is this the German U-boat thing?" Jas asked.

Michael nodded. "But Morgan didn't give any other details, so we are going in a little blind."

Our last assignment had gotten dicey in the end. While trying to uncover the reasons small atolls in the Gulf of Mexico were vanishing and affecting the oil exploration boundaries of Mexico, we'd drifted into a battle between corrupt government officials and bad private sector actors bent on corporate greed at all costs. What we ultimately uncovered put the Water Horse team in the crosshairs of violence. Rudy was recovering from a bullet wound to his shoulder, and to say that we were all operating in harm's way was an understatement. That had led Morgan to join an off the books team from Mexican intelligence to pursue and end the threat, permanently. I didn't like it, and I was worried. But I knew there'd been no other way that my former Navy SEAL brother, Morgan, would handle any threat to our family, our team, and our home. My former career as a conflict videographer had landed me in many dangerous environments and exposed me to the very worst examples of how groups of people could treat one another. I left that world, hoping to never again be knee deep in the ugliness. That's why I'd started Water Horse Expeditions. I wanted to dive and explore the world's oceans and serve as host to visiting (and paying) scientists and explorers. But me and our team found that bad actors could and do show up most anywhere. And my overriding desire to help people and communities victimized by greed and the need for power continually lead us into situations that most expedition boats rarely navigate. I was fortunate enough to have a crew that was as crazy as I was, and grateful for it.

With Morgan absent, we'd spent Christmas here in the Keys with my folks and our sister, Ellie, aboard the *Water Horse*. It was now mid-February. Mom and Dad were back in South Carolina and Ellie was back at her desk in New York City, working to break her next big news story. I was ready to get back to work as well.

The sun, warm breezes, and beautiful water were restorative, but it was hard to keep my worry at bay concerning Morgan. Although no one said it, I knew I was making the team crazy. After the New Year, I'd lead us into a marathon of scrubbing, painting, tightening and tweaking of every bolt and piece of camera gear on the boat. They were going to smother me in my bunk if I couldn't put us back to work on a new assignment soon. I hoped today's call would do just that.

I dropped the now folded shop rag onto the bench and turned to Jas. "Will you set up the video conference on the edit bay? And why don't you plan on sitting in on this one?"

She looked a little puzzled. "Jerry is first officer. Isn't he going to sit in?"

"Yeah, but I'd like you there as well."

After a short pause and eyebrow raise, she said, "I'll get the bay set up right away."

"Thanks," I said, as she headed to the hatch.

Jas had quickly become more than just our technology expert. She'd proven herself more than a few times in volatile situations. I'd decided that we'd use her personality and strengths in more of our decision-making process for upcoming assignments.

My phone chimed, and I rushed to dig it out of my cargo short's pocket. It was a text from Morgan.

You set for that call with NI?

If I could've reached through the electrons and smacked him, I would've. I texted back.

Yes. What's your status . . . asshat?

I got a smiley face emoji back, followed by, *Finishing up. You had the crew rub all the paint off the boat yet?*

I smiled, then typed: *Please get back soon so I can cane you with a boat hook.*

I waited anxiously for him to go for the electronic "last word," and he didn't disappoint.

Roger that, Brother. Pack a lunch.

Despite the adolescent brother jabbing, I was relieved to hear from him. Years before, when I was out on assignment as a conflict videographer in some war zone and he was on missions he could never talk about, I didn't remember worrying about him this much. These last few years, as we built a more connected life aboard the *Water Horse*, things had certainly changed in that department. Now, we were both a little older, a little more experienced, and I was worried. The afternoon passed quickly, and at five minutes before the hour, I stepped into the edit bay to find Jas sitting at the large console desk, configuring the giant LED screens for best viewing the encrypted video conferencing software that was forwarded to us, along with the invitation to the US Naval Intelligence call. Our first officer, Jerry Styles, had taken one of the leather easy chairs, leaving the remaining desk chair at the console for me.

"We about ready?" I asked.

"We are. The encryption code-ins for this video conference app are serious business," Jas replied. "Who's on the call for the Navy?"

"The email invitation said we'd be briefed by a commander, Edward Worley."

At precisely 3:00 p.m., the video window in the application blinked and popped into life and we were electronically face-to-face with who I assumed was Commander Worley. He looked to be in his early fifties, with a sea-worn complexion topped with a salt and pepper high-and-tight, heavy on the salt. His dress-white uniform held an impressive fruit salad on its shirt breast and his demeanor was exactly what you'd wish to have standing at your side on the bridge of a warship.

"Good afternoon, Commander Worley. I'm Michael Gannon and these are two of my team, first officer Jerry Styles and technology analyst, Jas Martin."

Jas gave me a subtle sideway look, having just been promoted to "analyst."

"Good afternoon, Captain Gannon. It's nice to meet you. Your brother, Morgan, has a sterling reputation within Naval Intelligence and now you're building quite the reputation for yourself."

"Thank you, Commander. I'm happy to ride my brother's coattails a bit. Our family is very proud of him," I replied.

"What we are about to discuss is highly classified information. I see that we've received the NDAs from your entire team. Are there any questions about the breadth of the disclosures you've signed?"

"No, sir, we're all very clear," I said.

"Good. Let's begin." The screen changed and the video image of Commander Worley popped into the corner and a black-and-white photo of a submarine tied to a dock filled the larger section of the screen. The photo was old and the men standing on the dock were wearing uniforms from the Second World War.

"This all begins near the end of the Second World War. German U-boats had inflicted massive damage to the Allied forces. It took almost two years to make any real defense against them."

The screen changed to a new photograph. Like the first, it was an old black-and-white, and the subject was again a submarine. It was like the first, but with noticeable differences in design.

"When Germany surrendered in 1945, they also surrendered a small fleet of new submarines so advanced that at that time, no practical defense against them existed."

The commander paused, and I looked at Jas and Jerry,

then back at the big screens. Worley continued. "These new subs, type XXI U-boats, were years beyond our design and capability and even further beyond the British. We were damned lucky only two of the boats left their bases and they were both surrendered before they saw any action."

"That was fortunate, Commander. I wasn't aware of that fact in naval history," I said.

"Few people are, but it's now more or less common knowledge among military history buffs. But this next piece of intelligence was not known by anyone in military intelligence until four months ago."

We all sat up a little straighter.

"In the chaos of the first week after the Berlin Wall fell, we secretly recovered a large cache of old archive documents dating back to the early 1940s. Anything that didn't scream Cold War or Russia got pushed into full archive status. But four months ago, an archivist scanning a load of documents for digital preservation ran across an old German naval communiqué with details on an operation known as 'Sleeping Wolf.' Luckily, the kid's father was CIA, and he had sense enough to call the Pentagon. The messages were cryptic, but once we had a few more clues about what to dig for, we found more bits and pieces of information about Sleeping Wolf scattered throughout the old documents. From what we've put together, it looks like they built just one boat of an even more advanced sub than the type XXI. This one-off prototype, code named X-601, possessed greater range, speed and firepower than the XXI. German engineers designed new coatings and anticorrosion seals, giving it the ability to stay submerged for extended periods of time."

"Commander, I take it, Germany did not include the X-601 prototype when it surrendered the other XXI class boats," I said.

"Not only was it not surrendered, we never had a hint it even existed until we discovered the old forgotten documents. It appears only weeks before Germany's surrender, the X-601 received orders to cross the Atlantic and enter the Gulf of Mexico. From the notes, the advanced boat could have remained submerged throughout most of the entire trip. The sub would then proceed up the Mississippi River as far as possible and launch its newly designed long-range V-2 rockets into the American heartland."

"Damn," Jerry said. "If they'd pulled that off, it would've changed the face of the war and history."

"You're right, Mr. Styles, it would have changed everything. But the most troubling part is the Sleeping Wolf angle of the operation. If the X-601 was detected before reaching its destination, the captain had orders to activate the Sleeping Wolf Protocol."

"I'm afraid to even ask," Jas whispered.

"If the 601 was detected, the Sleeping Wolf Protocol called for the sub to go deep, settle itself on the bottom, and wait."

"Wait? Wait for what?" I asked.

"The X-601 is supposed to be fitted with a special docking collar on its foredeck. Months, years, or even decades after the crew had expired, the designers of the X-601 conceived the idea of using its special access ring to allow another sub to dock, resupply, then complete its mission."

"It's the rise of the Fourth Reich," Jerry said from behind me.

We both turned to face him. "The true believer sickos within the Nazi Party all subscribed to this supernatural notion that a new Aryan super-nation would arise from the ashes of Germany's defeat. A 'Fourth Reich.'"

"You are correct again, Mr. Styles."

"Commander, these events may have taken place almost eighty years ago now. It's very interesting, but we don't even know if the X-601 made it across the Atlantic. Why is this a priority for Naval Intelligence now?" I asked.

"Commander, tell them about SC-412," Jerry said.

Jas and I both wheeled around in our chairs to stare at our shipmate that was revealing a formerly unknown military history . . . geek-ery.

"What?" he said. "Look, I was in Baltimore from right after high school until I joined Water Horse, but I'm a fourth generation Cajun. If you grow up on the Louisiana coast, there ain't much about the Gulf, the bayou, or the river you don't know."

The commander laughed. "Mr. Styles, why don't you tell us about SC-412, and if you miss anything, I'll fill in the gaps."

Jas and I fully rotated our chairs and faced our Cajun historian.

"Well, as the story goes, on a dark September night in 1944, the subchaser 412 was on patrol when another boat in the area reported what they guessed was a submarine snorkel being retrieved. The SC-412 under the command of Captain Walt Simpson detected the sub on sonar and began pursuing and dropping depth charges. After zeroing in on the sub's sonar reflection, they circled the position and increased their charges' depths settings and dropped two more volleys. The sub disappeared from sonar detection, and Captain Simpson reported they destroyed it, even though they detected no debris or oil slick. In 2014, when they discovered the wreck of U-166 off the coast of Louisiana, most people assumed it was a mix-up in history regarding which boat was where, as the PC-566 claimed to have sunk that sub."

"Your first officer is right on the money, Captain," said Worley.

I spun back around in my chair. "But again, Commander, what's causing the sudden urgency about an eighty-year-old sea battle?"

"For the last six weeks, we've been intercepting a great deal of chatter out of Europe concerning the keywords 'Sleeping Wolf,' along with coded numbers that, when configured as latitude and longitude coordinates, point to a dozen random positions eighty to one hundred miles off the Louisiana coast."

"That ramps the urgency up a bit," Jas muttered.

"Agreed," I said. "Commander, how can the Water Horse team help?"

"Captain, we need to find that sub before some bad actors try to restart it and pop up in New Orleans or Baton Rouge. And I'd like to do it without deploying an entire fleet of Navy ships that close to the mainland. That much naval activity would attract a lot of attention and probably induce panic. I can give you and your team two weeks until we'll have to initiate a full military operation. We can supply you with extensive satellite support and any experts you'll need."

"Understood, Commander. Let me brief my team, and I'll give you our answer in an hour."

Chapter 3

JAS CLICKED THE MOUSE and the video chat window closed on the screen. I turned to Jas and Jerry and said, "Well, what do you think?"

"Is it even possible, this many years later?" Jas asked.

"You could launch a small submersible off the back of an unsuspecting fishing boat and get to the sub if it's still intact," Jerry said. "I don't like the idea that a group of crazed neo-Nazis would even try to pull something like this off."

"Agreed," I said. "But even if the sub was destroyed and is inoperable, it'd still be an incredible discovery."

Jas repeated my last two words thoughtfully. "'Incredible discovery.' I like that phrase. You know I'm in."

I looked back at my first officer. "I'll have us fueled and paid up in a few hours. We can leave at first light tomorrow," Jerry said.

I wish Morgan was here for an assignment like this, but I know what he'd say. He tell me to pick up an extra door kicker from the commander and get to work. "Jerry, get us fueled, and I'll brief Beau and Rudy. We'll head to New Orleans at six a.m."

"Roger that, Captain."

"Jas, ring the commander."

Jas relaunched the encrypted video chat, and within a few seconds, Commander Worley was back on our screens.

"That was fast," Worley said, smiling.

"We're in, Commander. We'll leave at first light tomorrow. That'll put us in New Orleans in"—I did some quick math in my head—"a little under forty hours from now."

"Good," Worley said. "I took a chance on your answer and began uploading a full briefing package to a secure server. You can download it immediately. I'll also send you coordinates to an inactive ship terminal where you can dock, and we can bring you some useful tools and personnel."

"Roger that, Commander. We'll be underway first thing tomorrow."

Jas clicked us off the chat and turned to me. "The ROVs will definitely go into service, so I'm going to recheck those systems and have Beau help me stage them for launch. Can I do anything else to help?"

"Thanks for sitting in. I want your brain on more of these planning sessions."

"My brain is yours, Captain," Jas answered. And she left me sitting there in the edit bay, staring at the large electronic chart of the Gulf of Mexico that had been the screen saver on the large monitors since our last assignment. My brain fired into high gear on the first steps of our new assignment. Worley had committed some personnel to augment our crew, but no matter who he gave us, we'd still be a man down. Morgan should be here with us. He had more experience in this type of operation than anyone I knew. But more than that, he was my brother, and I desperately wanted him back in the fold of our team and our family.

I shook off my thoughtful daze and headed for the galley. I had a great shot of catching both Rudy and Beau there to brief them. My guess was correct. Rudy stood at the counter in the galley, putting the large top of a day-old biscuit over some bacon and handing it to Beau. It was his "Scooby-snack" for helping that morning. Beau was in his mid-thirties, but still ate like a teenage football player. Rudy often claimed, "The boy must have a tapeworm."

"Hey, glad I caught you two. We're headed for New Orleans at first light, as fast as we can paddle."

"Finally," Rudy said.

"Second that!" Beau said. "I thought we were going to polish the boat to death."

I held a raised eyebrow gaze at our deck boss, who quickly replied on cue. "But, man! The ship looks great, boss. And it'll be great to get back to work. What's our assignment?"

I smiled and let him off the hook a little. "We're going to help the Navy search for a World War II submarine off the coast of New Orleans. We'll do a full briefing over dinner tonight. Rudy, Jerry's arranging for fuel and settling our bill here at the marina. Do you need any help before we shove off in the morning?"

"No, sir. The gripe list in the engine room is clean as a whistle and we couldn't be more topped off and wrenched up if we tried. I'll use this bottomless pit of a marine here to help me put together a proper meal for our briefing."

"Excellent, I'll be in the pilothouse plotting a route. Pass the word, dinner and briefing at seven thirty. We shove off tomorrow at six a.m., sharp."

I left the galley and climbed the steps to the pilothouse. My previous rough calculations were pretty close. It was approximately five hundred eleven miles to one of the entrance buoys to the river. Then, depending on which ship terminal the commander would direct us to, that may add a few more miles. I downloaded the briefing packet that Jas had already loaded onto our ship's server and entered the coordinates to the ship terminal into the nav system. The total trip was five hundred sixteen miles. At our cruising speed of twelve knots, we would arrive at the terminal twenty-four hours after shoving off. I checked the weather for our Gulf passage and things looked calm. According to the forecast, winds would increase to eighteen knots by late the next day in the central Gulf, but the waves were expected to be only two to four feet, nothing that would slow us down.

I wrapped up my navigation prep and checked my watch. It was half past three. I had just enough time for a stroll and beer at the nearby watering hole and maybe a hogfish fingers basket. I passed Jerry on my way to the gangway.

"Be back by dinner, just going to go stretch my legs before we shove off tomorrow."

Jerry smiled. "Don't ruin your dinner with hogfish fingers."

Waving him off, I muttered, "Ahh." Clearly, I was becoming too predictable.

I loved it here on Stock Island. Our job always kept us on the move to our next assignment, wherever that took us. But, I was considering making this place our home base. That is, if I could find a spot for the boat that docking fees wouldn't break the bank.

It was an easy walk to the bar and grill. The old, weather-worn timber building with its palm frond roof had no doubt been doling out fresh fish and hydraulic refreshment for generations. My favorite seat at the far end of the bar was open, and I settled onto the stool with a relaxed sigh. The bartender sat a cold Heineken on a coaster in front of me and smiled.

"Am I that predictable, Sydney?"

"What? You want something else?"

"No . . . but. . . ."

"Billy, drop a fingers basket for me."

I just shook my head.

"There ain't nothin' wrong with knowing what you like, Michael. I always know what I like," she said with a playful smile.

Sydney was a third generation Keys local. She was tall, tan, and fit, with a beautiful long mane of sun-streaked blonde hair braided into a ponytail, pulled over one shoulder. Her deep tan made her blue eyes even bluer, and she had a tiny dimple in her left cheek that showed up when she flashed her full-lipped smile at you from across the bar. We'd flirted on and off the last few weeks, but it was just good clean fun.

"We're shoving off tomorrow, so I wanted one more fix of the hogfish."

"I'm sorry to hear that," she said. "Where you headed?"

"New Orleans."

"Mmm hmmm. A girl can get in lots of trouble in the Big Easy."

"So can a boy. But we'll be working, which may keep us out of trouble, part of the time. But I'd like to bring *Water Horse* back here after this assignment. You have any inside info on where we could tie up on a more long-term basis without selling a kidney?"

"Mmm, I'd like that," she said. Sydney seemed to mull it over as she carefully cut the lime slices that would garnish the multitude of house margaritas that she'd serve up a little later in the day. "You need to talk to old Randy Tyson. Supposed to be a cousin to one of the Tyson Chicken bigwigs. He bought stock early on and cashed out. Randy's got a custom woodworking shop, and his wife, Yvonne, makes pottery in that building down on the end of the basin. They've got a couple of hundred feet of seawall that stays open most of the time." She looked back at the old clock hanging on the wall. "Like a few of my other highly unpredictable customers, he'll be here in about six minutes."

"There's always one smart-ass in the group."

She smiled. "Just one of my many wonderful attributes."

The hogfish fingers arrived, and the perfectly portioned flaky white fillets were as heavenly as ever. I'd definitely miss my afternoons here. It'd been a nice spot to sit and think these last few weeks. But even with the gentle breezes, cold beer, and delicious hogfish, my heart knew it was time to get back to work.

A tall, slim man entered the bar area and took a seat two stools away. He had a gray beard and a Greek fisherman's hat covering a sun weathered head. Sydney put a Negra Modelo at his spot on the bar. Unlike myself, he didn't protest a bit, as Sydney perfectly anticipated his drink of choice. She looked down the bar at me and winked.

"Billy, drop another basket," Sydney called behind her. "Randy, this fella next to you is Michael Gannon. He's looking for a place to tie his boat up on a more regular basis. He owns *Water Horse*, that pretty navy-blue research boat over in the next basin."

The man extended his hand. "Nice to meet you, Michael."

"You as well, Randy. Sydney tells me you are a woodworker."

"Ahh, I still do small projects now and then. Seems like there's always a sailor needing something built or fixed on these old boats. Mostly it's an excuse for me and the wife to live on the water and for me to eat hogfish and flirt with Sydney here." We both laughed.

"What ya got in mind, Michael?"

"We're off tomorrow to work on a project up near New Orleans, but I think I'd like to base the operations of Water

Horse Expeditions out of Stock Island. Of course, we should be out on assignment most of the time but having a spot like this to regroup and heal after a long trip is kinda speaking to me."

"The sun, water, and breezes here make a good elixir for healin', that's for sure. When do you think you'll be back?" Randy asked.

"A few weeks, I would think."

"Well, if Sydney lets you sit at her bar more than once, you've passed muster, so give her a ring when you're headed back this way and we'll give it a try. How about that?"

I shook his hand. "That sounds outstanding, Randy. I'll do just that." I put a fifty on the bar and pointed to Randy's beer and hogfish. "Sydney, thanks so much. Keep a seat at the bar for me until I get back?"

She flashed a big, bright smile. "You know I will, Captain."

"Fair winds, Michael. Nice to meet you."

"You too, Randy." And I started back for the boat.

Jas was working on the aft deck and Harper was standing vigil at the rail gate as I climbed the gangway onto the main deck.

"Any trouble, Harper?" I asked our hairy sentry. His head leaned against my upper thigh for a rub, which I concluded meant "all's well" before making my way aft.

"Sydney have your beer waiting for you? She's a lot of woman, Michael," Jas chided.

"I'm only crazy about the fish fingers, and my hands are full right here with things on *Water Horse*," I said.

"Mmm hmm," she hummed.

"You need any help finishing up?"

"No, I'm good. Beau gave me a hand earlier. I'm glad we've got a new assignment. You think you can live without your fish fingers for a while?"

I pulled the brim of her ball cap down further over her eyes and turned for my cabin. "See ya at dinner."

"I'll be there," she called.

Chapter 4

RUDY AND BEAU OUTDID THEMSELVES with their preparation for our departure meal from the island. A bountiful combo of Keys' lobster tails and ribeye steaks. We all sat as heaping plates of mouth-watering food began the journey around the table. While everyone loaded their plates with surf and turf worthy of a food magazine spread, I raised my glass.

"To a needed rest, the swift return of our brother Morgan, and our new designation as a subchaser!"

"Hear! Hear!" came the calls from around the table.

"Subchaser?" Rudy asked.

"I'll fill you in during the brief," I said. "But I can tell you our first stop is the Big Easy at first light."

Crew meals were my favorite time of the day aboard *Water Horse*. The bonds we built around this table were growing stronger every time we sat here together. We stripped away the facade of our individual personalities around this table. We were becoming experts on each other's tempo, and with each passing day, we could all better predict each other's actions. This allowed us to operate together in a way that was at times akin to magic. But for me, the real reward was the new family that was forming and the new bonds that grew stronger each day.

After a few bites of the delicious meal, I began running through the information Commander Worley shared in our briefing that afternoon. The team sat wide-eyed as I revealed the existence of the surrendered advanced type XXI U-boats and the speculation of the one-off X-601 boat. Jerry retold the story of Captain Joe Hallsey and his reported but unconfirmed sinking of a sub while aboard the SC-412 that dark September night off New Orleans in 1944. From the additional material Worley uploaded to our servers, it was the Sleeping Wolf Protocol information that I wanted to fully unpack with the team.

"From the briefing material, it seems the designers of the X-601 included special advanced technology seals, air locks, and coatings that would theoretically allow the sub to stay purposely submerged on the bottom for extremely long periods of time. The designers incorporated a dark sacrificial aspect purposely and directly into the Sleeping Wolf Protocol. If the enemy detected the X-601 before it reached its objective, the protocol called for the crew to settle the boat on the bottom and then . . . expire."

Beau choked on a bite of green beans. "Expire?"

"Once the protocol was engaged, it was a suicide mission," I said.

The faces around the table fell somber.

"To what end?" Rudy asked.

Technicians designed a special docking collar on the main deck of the X-601. Upon Hitler's likely defeat the protocol would have staged the dormant sub for a new German faction in another submarine to enter the Gulf months, or even years later. That new sub could then dock with the X-601, resupply the boat and continue the 601's original mission."

"That's some crazy Fourth Reich nonsense," Rudy said.

"Except with the intelligence chatter coming out of central Europe, it didn't much sound like nonsense when Worley brief us this afternoon," Jerry replied.

"Admittedly, the whole idea seems a little far-fetched this many years after Germany's defeat. But I think the bit that rang my bell was the coded intercepts that contained LAT and LON numbers that marked twelve positions just offshore from the Mississippi River entrance."

"Hell's bells," Rudy muttered.

"What's Naval Intelligence want us to do?" Beau asked.

"They want us to find the boat before some swastika wearing jack-wagon does," Rudy answered for me.

"Well, yeah, that's basically it," I said. "But they also want to use us to keep from deploying a fleet of warships that close to the coast. Naval Intelligence feels it would attract too much attention and potentially cause panic."

"Panic?" Beau asked.

"Fifty-six Allied ships were sunk in the Gulf of Mexico during World War II, with very few of them being reported. The government leaned on the press hard not to report many of the U-boat encounters in the Gulf out of fear that it would cause panic. I'm not sure we're any less hysterical as a country eighty years later, so it's probably a good call," Jerry said.

"You seem to have a newfound expertise on Gulf Coast history for a Baltimore boy," Beau chided.

"It seems Baltimore Jerry was a multigenerational ragin' Cajun this whole time," I said.

"Oooo-wee! Don't dat pretty? Don't dat nice?" Beau rang out in a passable impersonation of the old "Cajun Cook" TV personality.

"You had to tell 'em, didn't you?" Jerry said to me while shaking his head.

"I didn't know it was a secret," I answered, realizing I may have started "a thing."

Jerry kept shaking his lowered head. "It'll be bad Cajun speak from him for weeks."

"Aw, come on, cher, I'm just messin' wit' ya," Beau cooed with an enormous smile.

In a full laugh, Jas choked out, "Oh! Do that one again."

Jerry just looked at me and stared, resigned to his fate, as the entire group rolled with laughter.

I raised my hand. "Okay, okay, give our boy a break. Let's finish up the brief and get some rack time. I want us pushed off no later than six a.m."

The laughter slowly subsided, and I continued. "We'll head to New Orleans and meet up with a Naval Intelligence team at an inactive terminal just off the river. Commander Worley promised some useful equipment and some extra hands until Morgan gets back."

"Then we go sub chasing?" Rudy asked.

"We do," I replied. "Jerry, what kind of water depths should we expect eighty miles off the entrance to the river?"

"Best I can remember, it'll be two hundred to as deep as four hundred feet, if we don't get out beyond the edge of the shelf."

"We can operate in those depths without any issues," Jas said.

"I agree," I said.

"What do we do if we find it?" Beau asked.

"If we find the boat, Worley will bring in a salvage team and the news will just be an antique discovery from the war. There'll be no mention of the Sleeping Wolf mission."

"Could a sub actually be operational after all these years?" Beau asked.

"It seems a little far-fetched, I admit," I answered. "But considering what we witnessed on our last job, then add the intercepted intelligence out of Europe, we have to consider it a real threat."

"Never underestimate a group of committed madmen," Rudy said.

"Or woman," I added.

The room fell silent as we each reflected on the ambition and greed of Mariana Vega, Mexico's former secretary of energy, that Morgan and a team of Mexican special forces were currently trying to bring to justice.

I stood to address the team. "Let's get some rest. All hands dressed and fed by five thirty. We'll cast off by six."

"Roger that, Captain," Jerry said as the rest of the team nodded in agreement.

As I made my way to my cabin, I pulled out my phone to check for an unlikely message from Morgan. Nothing. I typed a short text as I walked.

Water Horse bound for Big Easy at first light. Stay safe.

Once in my cabin, I opted for a hot shower. I knew I'd be up and moving by four the next morning, so I thought it may help me fall asleep faster. The hot water poured across the top of my head and down my back, easing the tension in my shoulders. My brain knew that I was facing a new reality of operating Water Horse Expeditions without Morgan, but my heart wasn't ready to accept it. I didn't know why, but down deep, I felt that Morgan and I were just getting started. Something special was gelling and growing on this boat, and Morgan was a huge part of it, and that's all there was to it.

I dried off and slipped on a pair of jeans before dropping into the chair at my desk. From the lower cabinet, I pulled out a glass and the bottle of Powers Irish whiskey that Dad left with me after our Christmas visit. Pouring a short shot, I lifted the glass and took a deep sniff of the Irish spirits. It was a little sharp on the nose, and it gave the back of my throat a pleasant, warm burn. A knock at my cabin door interrupted my little moment of bliss.

I opened the door and found Jas without her typical ball cap. Her long chestnut ponytail draped over one shoulder of the Water Horse Expeditions T-shirt that looked better on her than any other human, ever. Her olive skin was flawless with the smallest sprinkle of freckles across her nose and cheeks, and her long tan legs gracefully extended out of her cargo shorts, all the way to the floor. The daily look of Jas Martin was . . . perfection. She reached and pulled the perfectly weighted rocks glass from my hand. "Get your own." She smiled.

I stepped back as she stepped past me and dropped into the desk chair, swiveling it around to face the bed. I knelt beside her and retrieved another glass from the cabinet. When I stood, she was holding the bottle, and I held up my thumb and first finger, requesting a short pour. She complied, pouring the perfect amount. I raised my glass, and so did Jas, then I stepped back and sat on the end of my bunk.

"Anything?" she asked.

"No. I sent a message that we'd be underway at first light."

"He's a Navy SEAL. He'll find us," she said after a small sip. "Thanks for including me in the brief today. I liked it."

"Good thing. You're going to sit in more of them in the future."

Jas smiled. "If the Navy lends us some extra hands, can I use Beau to back me up on ROV ops?"

"Certainly."

"He's a damn good drone pilot and good tech, despite his jarheaded-ness."

I laughed. "I feel a little bad. He's going to torture Jerry with the Cajun thing."

45

"But only a little." She chuckled. "Too fun to feel very bad."

"True that," I said as I polished off the Powers.

"All right, I'm going to hit the rack," she said as she stood, stepping toward the door. "Thanks for the drink."

"Always," I said. Halfway through the door, I called to her. "Hey, Jas?"

She stopped and turned, looking over her shoulder at me.

"Good night."

"Night, Michael. Sleep fast," she said, smiling, and closed the door behind her.

I fell back onto my bunk, staring at the ceiling. Things between Jas and I had become more and more comfortable, but we hadn't jumped over that last fence. I'd been made aware that her last serious relationship ended poorly with her diving coach. So, as I lay there in my bunk with my imagination running amuck, crossing that line as her captain still had an air of 'ill-advised' to it. But something was happening between us, and the sense that we'd have to address it soon felt like standing on the tracks of an approaching train.

My alarm startled me awake at a quarter till four. I'd slept soundly and felt rested despite the insane hour. I slipped on a long-sleeved tee, jeans, and running shoes. Brushed my teeth and screwed on a Water Horse ball cap. It was church quiet in the harbor as I stepped out onto the port side main deck, opposite the dockside. The water was perfectly flat. As I stood looking out over the glassy still, a small ripple stirred on the surface and the utter quiet in the basin allowed me to hear the very human-like inhalation of a dolphin, taking a breath as it ghosted to the surface before quietly submerging on its quest for an early breakfast. It was one of the many little gifts of living on the water. These intimate little moments before the land-dweller world became too loud and too distracting. It is totally miraculous to witness a creature so completely and beautifully adapted to its environment.

The whiff of coffee brewing drifted through the still air, and I chuckled to myself. It was literally impossible to be awake before Rudy. I was beginning to think he was part horse and just slept standing up. As I stepped into the galley, he handed me an empty mug with what I remembered was his bad arm.

"Where's the sling, there, friend?" I asked.

"I decided my wing has healed enough," he said.

"I thought the doc said you had another week?"

"I'll arm wrestle you with it if I need to pass inspection," he said, pointing to the galley table.

I raised my hands in surrender. "Just some coffee for me, thanks."

Rudy butterflied both arms like an athlete stretching just before weightlifting. "Let's get this tub pushed off, and I'll whip up some two-armed bacon biscuits to power you through the first watch."

"Sold!" I said, as I filled my mug. "You and Jerry have the stern, and I'll have Jas and Beau on the bow this morning."

"You got it, Captain. I'm so ready to get back to work, I can hardly stand still." Harper signaled his agreement with a "woof!"

"I think that's the case for all of us. Time to get back out there. Start the mains when you're ready and I'll raise you on the radio when the team is in position." I turned to head to the pilothouse.

"Hey, Michael?"

I turned to our seasoned engineer.

"We'll be a full team again soon. I'm sure of it," he said.

I smiled and nodded. "Catch you on coms in a few."

Rudy smiled. "Aye, Cap."

I opened both wing doors in the pilothouse and allowed the early morning air to pass through. The harbor was just beginning to wake up, as a few fishermen prepared their boats to go to work. The excitement in my gut grew as the deck vibrated under my feet when Rudy started the main engine, bringing *Water Horse* to life. As I powered on the computer, radar, and nav instruments, my excitement intensified even more, knowing that the boat and her crew were getting back to what we were built for. With the final checks complete and the blooming glow of morning filling the eastern sky, I saw Beau and Jas step out onto the bow, ready to cast off. Beau raised his radio and his voice filled the pilothouse radio speakers.

"Lines are singled up, Cap. Ready when you are."

"Standing by on the stern," came Rudy's voice.

There was no current in the basin, so I could thrust the boat away from the dock and easily pull away. "Cast off the bow and stern and watch my clearances as I thrust us off," I said over the radio.

The thrusters whirred into action, causing the water to boil with turbulence between the hull and pier. Within seconds, the boat pushed away from the dock. When we were twenty-five feet from the dock, I released the thruster controls.

"Clear on the bow."

"Clear on the stern."

I engaged the transmission and *Water Horse* eased forward out of the basin. The morning sun was just peeking over the horizon as we made our way down the entrance channel, and within twenty minutes, our home/office was plying along in the calm water of the Florida Straits just under ninety miles from Havana, Cuba. We'd slowly ease westward in a few miles, followed by swinging all the way around to the northwest for the four hundred fifty nautical mile run to the Mississippi River entrance off New Orleans. Conditions were good. A big high pressure system nestled down on the entire northern Gulf, providing clear blue skies, small waves, and temperatures in the upper seventies. Living and working aboard a boat isn't all ice cream and rainbows. Mechanical failures, bad weather, and things that need scrubbing and paint, fill many of your days. But like my treat encounter with the dolphin earlier in the morning, there are moments and conditions that induce powerful pain-and-suffering amnesia, and this was another example.

With the fresh morning breeze pushing through the open pilothouse doors, I sat back in the big pilot seat and propped my feet up onto the teak dash trim on either side of the ship's wheel. My shoulders relaxed and an almost audible thought ran through my mind. *At this very moment, it doesn't get much better than this.*

Rudy's voice across the radio startled me out of my boat owner "amnesia."

"Anybody want a bacon biscuit?"

I relaxed again . . . amnesia intact.

Chapter 5

BY MIDDAY, WITH THE CONDITIONS holding steady, Jerry relieved me at the helm. There wasn't much to do other than monitor the ship's instruments and watch for boat traffic. But letting your guard down on a long, calm run had spelled ruin for many a mariner. The crew would stay sharp and everyone wanted helm time on a day like today.

"A bearing of three-o-eight for another three hundred sixty miles," I said.

"Roger that, Cap. A long straight line and plenty of deep water," Jerry said. "Beau will relieve me in four hours. That'll put us at the terminal late in the day, tomorrow."

"That's what the computer says," I answered. "Between three and four p.m. depending on traffic in the channel."

"Then take a break. I got her, Michael."

"I'm gonna dig a little deeper into the brief that Commander Worley uploaded to us. This whole thing is a hell of a sea
story."

"One thing's for sure, Cap, it's never boring aboard this
boat."

I shook my head and smiled. "Nope, we don't do boring
very well. Shout if you need me. I'll be in my cabin."

"Roger that."

Sitting at my desk, I opened my laptop and did a quick
email check. Nothing new. No message from Morgan. I dou-
ble clicked the folder from Worley and combed through the
documents and intel briefs that Worley's team had been col-
lecting the last few months. There was a significant amount
of intercepted chatter around Operation Sleeping Wolf, but I
was interested in knowing more about the original crew of
the X-601. The captain of the advanced boat was Hans
Schreiber. Schreiber received many high decorations from
the German Navy. His reputation was sterling, and the three
U-boats he commanded during the war were responsible for
torpedoing over twenty enemy ships, sending them to the
bottom.

There was a picture of Schreiber in the file and I clicked
it to enlarge the image on the laptop screen. The photo was
exceptionally clear. The man appeared to be in his late thir-

ties, just a little older than Morgan and me. Schreiber stood tall and thin but equally strong and athletic, with a square jaw and the intense stare of a serious man. The veteran sub captain possessed a look of a tough, capable seaman that I, for one, wouldn't savor going to battle against, especially in an advanced German U-boat. The more I looked through the files, the more curious I became. Schreiber would have known Sleeping Wolf was a suicide mission. Then further digging revealed something that shed some light on why such a decorated captain would step forward for this kind of mission. In the winter of 1942, an Allied bomb meant for a weapons factory near their village of Friedrichshafen missed its target and hit near his home, killing his young wife, Sophie and daughter, Anna. While Schreiber battled a war at sea to defend the motherland, he was helpless to defend the very reason he fought.

I stopped scrolling and sat back in my chair. The senseless loss of a wife and child would be hard for any man to take. And to be away at sea with no way to return. I couldn't imagine his grief. Schreiber was on the wrong side of a war and the wrong side of history, but he was equally a husband and a father.

A news headline alert bubble popped up onto my screen. I clicked it and the headline story filled a larger window. The headline read: "Corrupt Mexican government officials taken into custody after an intense gun battle in a mountainous region of the country."

I frantically read through the text of the story. Morgan's infrequent texts let me know he was still alive, but never any details as to his mission's status. As it goes with most breaking news stories, the details were scant. I was confident no one would identify him by name, but I hoped for a clue as to his location. The brief article revealed that four former Mexican officials were in custody and that there were casualties among the group of fleeing officials, their protection team of guerrilla fighters, and the military taskforce executing the mission to apprehend the fugitive officials. The article contained no details regarding the exact number of casualties, much less any names. There was also no mention of Secretary of Energy Vega, so it was impossible to know if she was even there. Morgan had insisted on doing this mission because Vega tried to ambush our boat and kill our crew. She'd shown an intent to continue her hunt until she eliminated anyone that could implicate her and her accomplices in the massive oil exploration conspiracy in the Gulf. I checked my phone again for a message from Morgan. Still nothing.

I got up and stepped into the head, splashing water on my face from the sink. I knew I couldn't sit here all afternoon. If I did, I'd go crazy. So I headed for the camera shop.

Descending two decks and stepping into the compartment, I found Jas with one of our ROVs we called Woody, perched up on the workbench.

"Hey, Michael, what's the news?"

"Funny you asked that, I just had a news headline pop up on my laptop about a major takedown of corrupt Mexican officials with casualties on both sides."

Jas's smile fell away, and she put her screwdriver on the bench. Her face turned pale. "Any names or details?"

"No," I said.

"No mention of Vega?" she asked.

"Nothing."

Jas paused, then turned back to the ROV and picked up the tool and began adjusting the mount on a new instrument that she'd added to the drone's front face. "He's fine," she said with a little too much "chipper" in her voice to sell it completely. "He's going to show up any day now, and his first day back, he'll want us in sparring training before dinner."

I walked over to the bench and leaned against it. "You're right, he will. And I hope he's so tired that I beat him like a drum."

Jas stepped closer, leaned against me, and whispered, "Never gonna happen. But I love your little dream."

"Hey, I've gotten close a few times."

Jas patted me on the back like a coach comforting the kid

who just dove and missed the catch at first base. "Let me show you Woody's new eyes," she said as she slipped back into work mode.

I turned to face the ROV. The new gear mounted on the front of Woody resembled a set of white cartoonish eyes. The six-inch-round half spheres sat side by side just above the front-facing 8K camera.

"This is a new high intensity compact sonar array or HIC-SA for short," she said, pointing to the two bulges. "In the right conditions, the resolution of this new scanning tech produces sonar images rivaling an actual video image. And eighty percent higher resolution than traditional sonar in water conditions with high turbidity from silt and particulates. HIC-SA will enable us to see things far beyond the range of what the cameras can see."

"Wow, where did this come from?" I asked.

"An old classmate from Georgia Tech called around Christmas. He was excited about the technology but frustrated he hadn't been able to find a research team willing to put the gear into the field for testing. A week later, two shipping crates arrived at the dock on Stock Island and wa-la, we've got some exciting new tech for finding dangerous sleeping subs."

I noticed a few printed pictures on the workbench and I picked one up for a closer look. It was an image of a ship's bow in deep, dark water. The detail of the biological growth encasing the bow rails and other structures on the sunken vessel were clearly visible. It was almost as clear as underwater photos I'd seen during my diving career. "Are these images from the HIC-SA?" I asked.

"Yep. Pretty impressive, yeah?"

"This almost looks like a full video image. That's amazing," I said.

"A team recorded that image in seven hundred feet of water, and because it's sonar, not optical, it didn't require any light. It was pitch black at that depth."

"If HIC-SA works this well for our mission, it'll be invaluable," I said, looking through the other printed images on the bench.

"I agree. I don't think it'll replace the need for real video and photos, but there are situations when this will give us much more capability to see what's happening at depth."

"What did it cost us?" I asked.

"Nothing for now," Jas said. "Ted just asked that we document our experience with the gear. If we like it, he said we could work something out to keep it."

"This mission is highly classified. We can't share anything about what we're doing, much less share any images we capture with this tech. Will that burn a bridge with your friend?"

"I'll take care of Ted," she said, smiling.

Despite my effort to hide it, the look on my face must have changed, because she quickly added, "I'll dive on some harmless targets before we leave the area and record all the data. That'll satisfy Ted's team."

"Gotcha," I said. "I can't wait to see it in action. The scanner domes really add a face to our boy Woody here."

Jas smiled. "Yeah, I'm trying to resist the urge to paint on some black pupils and eyelids for looks."

I chuckled as I checked my watch. "I wish that bonehead of a brother would hit me with a message."

Jas reached and touched my arm. "He will, Michael. Give him a little more time. He's okay, I can feel it."

"I'm glad you do," I said. "You'll need to feel it enough for both of us for now."

"I can do that," she said. "But now, I've got work to finish up, so go away. Go bug Rudy or stand another helm watch. Keep yourself busy, and I'll check in with you this evening."

I opened my mouth to say something, but she'd already turned back to her work. I just closed my mouth, smiled, and turned to head for the pilothouse.

The day and early evening passed quietly. Helm watches changed, and we all fed ourselves when we could on sandwiches and leftovers that Rudy kept stashed in the freezer. At midnight, I was lying in my bunk rereading an old Travis McGee novel when a knock on my door brought a smile to my face. I jumped to my feet and stepped to the door, confident it was Jas for her promised "check." I opened the door wearing a big stupid grin, only to be greeted by the serious, then quizzical face of Beau Benson.

"Ah . . . evening, Cap. You might want to come check this out."

I followed Beau to the pilothouse. There were enough moonlight for decent visibility on the water and conditions were calm. Jerry was back at the helm and Jas stood out on the port side wing deck with a pair of night vision binoculars.

"I started marking an intermittent target on the radar about a half hour ago. I knew it wasn't a boat, it was moving too fast," Jerry reported. "There's no AIS signature and no radio traffic."

"What's our position?" I asked.

"We're one hundred and ninety miles off the outer sea buoy near New Orleans," Jerry said, confirming his answer with the information on the nav screen. "And maybe seventy miles from what will be our search area."

"There!" Jas called. "Four hundred yards off the port bow, heading northwest about eighty feet off the surface. It's a drone, a pretty big one."

We all looked over her shoulder in the direction she pointed, but it was too far and too dark to see the unmanned aircraft with the naked eye. Jas handed me the binoculars, and as I struggled to pick out the target in the dark sky, a bright neon green scanning laser blinded me as it overpowered the electronic night vision of the optics. I slammed my eyes shut, trying to adjust and regain my sight. When I looked up, I could clearly see the laser extending from the dark flying object as it scanned across the surface of the Gulf, flying a roughly parallel course to ours, heading northwest.

"What in the hell is that?" Beau asked.

Even at this distance, Harper stood with his front paws on the deck rail, alternating between a bark and a low growl directed at the strange object.

"It's doubling back," Jas said, as the laser stopped scanning and the aircraft banked sharply to the east, then southeast. Its laser resumed scanning the surface of the water, covering an area that appeared to be about one hundred fifty feet across. As it closed to within two hundred yards of our position, we could hear the high-pitched whine of the rear props powering the drone. The dark shape of the winged bird was going to cross our course a hundred yards ahead. Jas scrambled to the pilothouse and ran back out on the wing deck with the digital camera and long lens just before the craft crossed our position. She triggered a series of bursts, capturing images of the ominous craft and its scanning laser as it streaked by.

"Does it look like one of ours?" I asked.

"Not like any I'm aware of," Jas answered. "Beau, how about you?"

"Looks similar to a MQ-9 Reaper, but the tail section is all different. Then there's the laser. That's a new wrinkle."

"Damn," I said. "I'd hoped we'd have some kind of head start."

"Maybe it's one of Worley's," Jas said.

"Maybe," I said.

"I'll get these pictures into the bay and see if I can process some details into the images."

"He's doubling back again," Beau said as he watched the drone from the starboard side wing deck.

The black drone and laser were further to the east of our position on this pass but still headed in our general direction. When the aircraft reached a point two miles northwest of us indicated by the small faint reflection on the radar, the bright green scanning laser stopped and any trace of the drone disappeared. I looked at my watch. It was almost one in the morning. I pulled my cell phone from my pocket and dialed the number. Someone picked up the call on the third ring.

"Worley here. What's your eta, Captain?"

"We'll be in by four p.m.," I answered.

"We'll be ready for you."

"Commander, any chance Naval Intelligence is running drones outside the search area?"

A long silence was his only reply.

"I'll have images when we arrive. Looks like someone's already looking for our Sleeping Wolf."

"Roger that, Captain. I'll see you at the dock."

Chapter 6

THE COMMERCIAL BOAT TRAFFIC in the Mississippi River channel was heavier than I expected as *Water Horse* wound through the twists and turns marked by the red and green navigational markers. Even though the blue water of the Gulf had now transitioned into the brown sediment filled river, the Mississippi's rich sense of history had a beauty all its own. The green and browns of the tidal marshes stretched out of sight in every direction. My imagination conjured up stories of the ships from every corner of the globe that had navigated this channel for centuries before us, making their way into the port of New Orleans for commerce and trade. The pirate stories of faraway tropical ports may appear in more books and movies, but these waters have been witness to just as much intrigue, mischief, and eye-patch-wearing customers as any seaport in the world.

We easily located the abandon terminal cut into the east bank of the river, and Jerry slowly steered us into the facility's entrance. I stood next to him in the pilothouse as he masterfully maneuvered our hundred and forty feet of steel deeper into the terminal basin.

"How's it feel to be back home?" I asked.

"I'm a little ashamed it's been so long. I call my folks often, but that's not the same. There's a load of cousins that I was close with when I was younger. I didn't mean to stay away, ya know. Life just seemed to happen. You wake up and suddenly it's been a few years instead of a few months."

"Don't be too hard on yourself. We've all been there. Let's get you ashore for some time to catch up when we wrap this up."

"I'd like that, Michael. Thanks."

As Jerry eased *Water Horse* into the back of the terminal basin, the only sign of human activity anywhere around the forgotten-looking facility appeared to be two military cargo trucks parked near the edge of the dock. Jerry pulled *Water Horse* alongside the pier, and a half a dozen men dressed in plain clothes emerged from what looked like an abandon rusted metal building ten yards from the end of the basin.

The men rushed to catch the dock lines, ready to be tossed by Beau and Jas. In minutes, the men had us secured to the dock. Together, Jas and Beau lifted our gangway steps into place as I made my way down from the pilothouse and out onto the main side deck with Jerry in tow. I motioned for Jas and Jerry to follow me, and Jas handed me a manilla folder as we started down the gangway steps. I spoke to the first man we approached on the dock.

"Commander Worley?" I asked.

The man pointed toward the metal building, and the stout, balding man that was already walking in our direction. He wore a short-sleeved plaid button-up shirt and a pair of tan kakis. He may have been Naval Intelligence now, but earlier in his career, this man had spent many years aboard ship. You could just see it. His weathered face held the lines of experience and crow's feet, earned from squinting across countless sunbaked seaways. Extending my hand, I said, "Commander Worley?"

"Captain Gannon," he said as we shook.

I looked down at his forearm and caught a quick glimpse of USMC and USS *Enterprise* tattoos, now faded with age.

"Michael is fine," I said. "This is Jas Martin and Jerry Styles."

"Nice to meet you both. Do you have pictures for me?" Worley asked, getting right down to business.

I handed the commander the folder from under my arm, and he opened it quickly to examine the photographs.

Jas stepped forward. "I was able to pull out some additional detail with our software, but I couldn't find any visible markings on the drone."

Worley nodded while studying and flipping through the collection of images. "Looks like there's a radar defeating coating on the fuselage."

"There's no way it could be one of ours?" I asked.

"I'm afraid not," Worley said, shaking his head in disappointment. "But after seeing these images, I think we can retune our radar scanning to be more discriminating. And I have a few pieces of equipment that I think will give you and your team an edge out there. Let's get 'em loaded, then we'll feed you and the crew before we put you back to sea."

Worley pointed toward the two military trucks with their tall canvas-covered cargo areas and we all walked in their direction. As we approached the rear of the first truck, any clue to its cargo remained hidden by the canvas curtain hanging over the rear opening.

"Take a look," Worley said, motioning for me to pull back the curtain.

I reached and lifted the canvas flap to the side. There, yawning and stretching, sat a shaggy and unshaven Morgan Gannon on the side-mounted bench. He blinked hard as he peered out of the dark cargo area, trying to adjust his eyes to the light.

"Hey, Brother! You got a spare rack on that tub? I need a place to crash."

I grabbed his arm and yanked him out of the truck, depositing him on his feet on the dock.

"You really need to learn to use a phone," I said as I pushed him in the chest, knocking him backward. The group laughed, then he pulled me into a tight hug.

"You had me scared," I said softly.

"I know. But it's over. No one from the Vega camp will come."

I pulled back, holding him at arm's length to look him in the eyes.

He nodded at me again. "It's over."

I nodded back, grateful for the news, but more relieved that anything we'd face in the future, we'd face as a team. "It's the last time you'll leave me behind, Brother. Are we clear?"

Morgan's smile faded, and he glanced down for a second before meeting my eyes again with sincere acceptance. "Roger that. It's you, me, and the team."

I pulled him into another hug as the rest of the team closed in to welcome our brother back into the fold.

"Incoming!" Rudy called, as the group turned to see

Harper in a full run toward us from his position at the top of the gangway. Reaching Morgan, he jumped, placing his front paws on Morgan's chest, and thoroughly drenched his face with licks.

"Hey, Harper! Good to see you too, buddy," Morgan said, trying to dodge the lapping tongue.

Rudy stepped up and slapped Morgan on the back. "I bet you're a fella that'd enjoy a meal that didn't end with MRE! I'll take care of that. Glad to have you home, Morgan."

There was more laughter and handshakes as Beau and Jerry added their welcomes. Then, as the excitement faded, Jas stepped in to embrace Morgan. "Can we have one more day off before we train again?"

"Oh, my brother's been letting you guys get soft, has he?"

"Nah, it'll just be the first restful night's sleep we've had in a while," Jas said, smiling. "We're glad you're home, Morgan."

My brother nodded slowly, acknowledging the deeper meaning of her words, then in a false bravado declared, "I guess a few more days can't hurt. Some of Rudy's cooking and a night in my rack won't hurt, either."

I pushed him on the shoulder, causing him to stumble to the side before catching his balance. "Better sleep fast, slick. We've got a sub to find."

Morgan chuckled and turned back to me. "Yeah, the commander briefed me this morning."

Worley stepped back into the family circle, ready to get back to business. Morgan looked at the old Naval Intelligence officer. "Any more intel on the drone the crew spotted last night?"

Worley shook his head. "Nothing other than it's not ours. But let's show 'em what else we've got," he said, pointing to the other cargo truck.

As a group, we moved over to the second truck and its covered cargo bed. The commander stepped up to the rear curtain and flipped it up over the top, revealing the prize inside. A large, gleaming Lexan bubble filled the entire rear of the cargo box.

"That looks just like a smaller version of . . ."

"The *Sea Eye*," Morgan said, finishing my sentence. "Kyle and Sid designed a smaller version of their submersible for the Navy."

Kyle Bennett and his senior engineer Sid Melson of the ocean research firm, Sea Watcher, were old clients and friends from a past assignment. Their team was pivotal to us uncovering and ending the cause of nine billion red king crab vanishing from the Bering Sea. *Sea Eye* was their highly advanced submersible that could carry a crew of three, but this version seemed much smaller and meaner.

"It's a two-man version," Morgan said. "But this design has a few more teeth than the research-only version."

"What's that mean?" I asked.

"Let me show you," Worley said, as he flipped down the tailgate of the cargo box and pulled a lever. With a click, the floor of the cargo bed slid outward from inside the canvas-covered area and into the open. Seconds later, we all got our first glance at a far more menacing version of the larger *Sea Eye* submersible that we were familiar with.

"What! Are those mini-torpedoes?" Beau asked, pointing to the side-slung launcher devices mounted on each side of the flat-black painted frame.

"They are," Worley said. "Six heat-seeking, armor-piercing mini-torpedoes. It has increased range, it can operate deeper, and it runs tetherless with an advanced sonar-wave communication system back to the mother ship. We call it *Sinbad*."

"Love that," Jas cooed.

Slung low under the observation bubble was a metal ring structure that extended down from the main cockpit space twenty-four inches.

"Is that a docking collar?" I asked.

"It is," Worley said. "It's a shot in the dark that it'll match up with the collar that's supposed to be on the 601. They didn't design *Sinbad*'s collar for this mission. It was designed for two-man SEAL Teams to launch off one of our subs. We're hoping we'll get lucky."

"Who drives?" I asked.

"I do," a voice said from behind us.

We all turned to see the stout-looking man none of us had seen approach our group. He had a square jaw with a text-book salt and pepper high-and-tight haircut. He wore navy-blue BDU trousers and a gray T-shirt covering the torso of a lean-muscled mariner.

"Mac Summers," he said, extending his hand to Morgan, who stood closest to him. "You're Morgan Gannon."

Morgan shook the man's hand. "Yes, sir."

"Your reputation within the Teams precedes you. And this must be your brother, Michael," he continued, reaching to shake my hand. "I've heard of you as well, Captain."

Surprised, as we shook, I said, "Well, I never know if that's good or bad, but nice to meet you, Mac."

"All good, Michael," he said, as the group laughed. "Are you willing to put me and *Sinbad* to work?"

"Tough job ahead, so we'd be glad to have you, Mac."

"Who rides the rear seat?" Beau asked, almost visibly vibrating with anticipation.

"You have any suggestions?" Mac asked.

"I've got a hundred hours piloting a larger DSVR," Beau said, as he looked at me like a teenager asking to drive the car for the first time.

It seems our former marine continued to surprise us regularly with new skills he seemed to reveal out of the blue. He was a former member of the Sea Watcher crew. While working in Alaska, he'd really clicked with our team. Then, with Kyle's blessing, we offered Beau a permanent position with the Water Horse family. Since then, he had proven himself an accomplished drone pilot, ROV driver, mechanic, and an excellent marksman. Beau spoke little about his time in the Marines, but he'd become invaluable to us in the last year and his actions continually proved him to be a good man. So when he was ready to tell us more, I knew he would.

After I closed my gapping mouth, I asked, "You drive anything else you've not told us about?"

"Ah . . . maybe?"

I looked at Morgan. "Beau was going to back Jas up on ROV ops. You good to fill in there?"

"I'm not itching to crawl in that thing. So, yeah," Morgan said, nodding.

"Well, Mac, he has awful jokes, and you may need a shoehorn to get his overgrown self into the rear seat, but if you can use the help, you couldn't do better."

Mac stepped over to shake Beau's hand. "Nice to meet you, Beau. We'll start getting you checked out in the *Sinbad* as soon as we're loaded and underway."

"Roger that," Beau said. "Looking forward to it."

"Okay, let's get you loaded," Worley said, raising his arm

in a circling motion, kicking off a flurry of activity among the other men on the dock.

One group of men retrieved four pelican cases that were in the truck, where we found Morgan, and made their way to our gangway steps. Rudy helped them transfer the cases onto our side deck. Then a motorized truck crane emerged from the rear of the metal building and in short order, Worley's team had the intimidating looking *Sinbad*, along with its cradle, ready to lift. The crane raised *Sinbad* up and over our stern rail and into its temporary nest on *Water Horse*'s aft deck. Jerry directed the crane operator as Jas guided the submersible into place, allowing Mac and Beau to secure the tie-down straps into the deck rigging points.

Commander Worley, watching the loading process, leaned over and bumped against me, getting my attention. "*Sinbad* looks good sitting on your aft deck, Captain."

"It's a tough-looking fish for sure," I said.

"Let's get you and your crew fed and on your way. We've got a spread set up inside."

I whistled to get the crew's attention and motioned for them to come back ashore as I pointed toward the large metal building.

Once our crew assembled, I led as we stepped into the entrance of the building that on the outside appeared ready to collapse under its own weight. I stopped abruptly after only two steps inside. I stood completely taken aback by the shocking deception pulled off by the outer appearance of the old, rusty building. The interior was well lit and ultra-modern in every detail. Along the far back wall, aligned in two separate rows, were a dozen workstations equipped with computers and advanced electronic monitoring equipment. On the right-hand wall, there were glass divided offices buzzing with activity. On the opposite wall, there were maybe a dozen small bunk rooms. Out in the center of what I guessed to be the eighty-by-eighty foot space stood a large briefing table. Even that was a surprise, because the entire top surface was an electronic display currently filled edge to edge with a chart of the Gulf of Mexico with an overlay of active ship and aircraft tracking telemetry updating live on the screen.

The rest of our crew must have internally shared my mental reaction because, for the first time, maybe ever, they all stood silently gawking at the impressive op center in front of us.

"Whaddya think of our humble digs?" Worley asked as he turned to look at our shocked faces.

"Whoa," Beau blurted out.

"That about covers it," I added. "Not sure I could come up with anything better."

"We cover intel for all the Gulf of Mexico and as far west as the Dominican Republic," Worley said proudly.

"You're well disguised, that's for sure," I said.

Worley smiled. "I'll give you the full tour after we've towed that sleeping sub into this terminal. But now, let's eat and get you shipped out."

Across from the high-tech briefing table sat several round tables and chairs, and beyond that, a hearty buffet awaited our team. None of our crew wasted any time digging into the steaming selection of barbecue ribs, chicken, and fresh vegetables. We'd just sat down to eat when a chiming alarm pinged from the interactive briefing table. One of the op center techs walked quickly to the table and began manipulating the chart image on the surface. The operator looked to Worley, urging him to approach the table. I swallowed my first bite of potatoes and invited myself to follow the commander.

"What do we have, Tim," Worley asked the young technician.

"A fast-moving target just popped up within our search grid."

The tech pointed to a blue dot that appeared and disappeared as it moved across the chart of the Gulf."

"Is that our drone?" I asked.

"It's not broadcasting an aircraft identification signal, and it's too fast for a boat."

"Why is it blinking on and off?" I asked, as we all closely watched the target appear for a few seconds, then vanish.

"It's flying very low," Worley said. "We've retuned our sensors, so if that's your drone, I'm glad we can see it at all. If it descends too close to the surface, we'll lose it again."

As if a drone pilot somewhere could hear our conversation, the dot moving across the electronic chart blinked once more, then disappeared from the screen.

"Damn," Worley grunted. The commander turned to the group as they ate. "Eat up, men. We gotta move."

Chapter 7

JERRY WAS AT THE HELM, navigating *Water Horse* out of the dark terminal channel and communicating with Jas and Beau on the radios as they stood watch out on deck. Beau's voice came across the radio and into the pilothouse speakers. "Jerry, there's an unlit set of pilings off the next point to port. Can you see that?"

"Got it, but keep calling out everything you see," Jerry replied.

Morgan and I stood nearby at the chart table, studying Worley's best estimates for a grid area where we should start our search.

I pointed a portion of the chart about seventy miles due

south of the first entrance buoy to the river entrance. "I've read the intel and the translated memos that were uncovered in the archives a dozen times. Even with all that, it's still a guess. Nevertheless, I think we should start here, at this point in the commander's grid, and search due east."

"I'll take an informed guess anytime," Morgan said.

Continuing, I traced my finger across the chart along the first track I proposed we search. "We can use the ship's sonar first, then if we hit anything interesting, we'll launch Woody for a closer look. Wait till you see the new sonar array mounted on him. Jas has it on loan from a research team friend at Tech. It's pretty impressive. They're calling it HIC-SA. High intensity, compact sonar array. Thing looks like Woody has a set of bug eyes."

"Look forward to seeing that in action," Morgan said.

I looked at my watch and over at the navigation screen. "Jerry, looks like we'll be on station between three and four in the morning. You agree?"

"That's what I'm thinking," Jerry said. "Unless we get slowed down dodging river traffic on our way out of the channel."

"When we get clear of the outer marker, let's run eight to nine knots on our way out. I know we'll end up working in the dark at some point, but if we run a little slower on the way out, we can get started at first light tomorrow."

"Roger that," Jerry said. "Beau is relieving me at twelve. I'll brief him on that when he takes the helm."

Morgan yawned and scratched his scruffy beard. "I'm going to shower, shave, and get some sleep."

"That sounds well deserved. And we'd all appreciate the first two tasks on the list," I said.

"Nice," Morgan answered.

"You're welcome," I said. "I'll relieve Beau at four. You sleep in and I'll have somebody rattle your bunk when we're on station ready to run the first leg of the search grid."

Morgan started for the steps out of the pilothouse, and before he cleared the hatch, I called to him, "Hey, Morgan?"

He turned to face me. "Yeah?"

"Welcome home."

Morgan smiled. "Good to be home, Brother." And he disappeared through the hatch.

"Why don't you grab a nap too, Cap," Jerry said. "You may actually sleep a little, now. I've got a feeling we're going to have some long days ahead. Drones, rouge subs, and Eurotrash terrorists? This fandango is off to a fast start this time."

"That's a great prelude to sleep. Thanks," I said, chuckling."

"Sorry," Jerry said, with his head lowered a little. Then he brightened. "It ought to be fun finding that sub, though!"

79

"We definitely need to find it before someone else does. Yell if you need me, I'm out."

"Will do, Cap."

In my cabin, I showered, brushed my teeth, and slipped on a pair of jeans and T-shirt. I always slept in my clothes when we were underway. You never knew when there'd be an alarm bell signaling a mechanical failure. Or something encountered on helm watch that would require quick rousing and action. You should always tackle those things in more than your skivvies. I reached and flipped off the bedside lamp before collapsing in a heap onto my bed. I was tired enough to fall asleep instantly. But instead, I lay there, staring at the ceiling, contemplating the potential dangers our team was about to dive into. Here we were again. Were we chasing elusive sea life or capturing footage of beautiful re-generated coral reefs? No, we were looking for an eighty-year-old German sub that terrorists were trying to recover in order to launch an attack on the American heartland. I almost laughed out loud to myself. But then, something else happened. A strange sensation washed over me. I could only describe it as relief, like a weighted blanket was lifted off my chest and then a release in the tension of my neck muscles. I'd felt it before in my conflict videographer days. It seemed to happen after crawling out of some nightmare environment. I'd be taking fire all day, bunkered in a shelter, embedded with military forces. Then I'd have to turn off my emotional brain to capture footage of the aftermath of some bloody battle, that seemed rather pointless after the fact. Sometimes it was hours or even days later when my brain was ready to ask, Hey, what happened out there? The emotional reflection often came with some pretty strange physical sensations. While lying there, I guessed, with all the earlier activity at the terminal, my body had once again filed Morgan's safe arrival into the "process later" basket. But now, here in the quiet, the realization that Morgan was safe and back aboard *Water Horse* was like a dip in an emotional Jacuzzi. I felt the physical effects of the blessing, and I was intensely grateful.

My phone pinged, startling me. I reached for it on the bedside table and saw it was a text.

You up?

I typed a one thumb response.

Yep.

My cabin door opened quietly and closed again. Jas fell across the bed sideways, her head settling to rest against my stomach.

She gave a long exhale, relaxing into her position. "Feel better, now that he's home?" she asked quietly in the dark.

"I do."

"Me too," she said.

The feel of her head against me and the warmth of her closeness, eased throughout every muscle like heated oil. The subtle curtain of awkwardness that separated us when we were alone was gone, and I felt no need to fill the silence. We just laid there, sharing the quiet. My eyelids were getting heavy as the day's events and the anticipation of what tomorrow may bring began slipping further and further into the back of my mind. From that little hazy spot just between awake and asleep, I heard her voice say, "Just rest a little now."

At a quarter till four, my phone alarm chimed, and I reached quickly to silence it, not wanting to wake Jas. But I found myself alone in the bed. I had slept soundly for almost six hours. Other than the blanket draped over me, I didn't remember having when I laid down, there was no sign of her. I put on some running shoes, pulled on a ball cap, and headed for the pilothouse. In my predawn stumble, I forgot to stop in the galley for a coffee that I'm sure Rudy had kept brewing all night for the crew. I stepped into the pilothouse and found Beau in the helm chair with his feet propped up on the console.

"Hey, ça va, cher, Captain?"

"What?" I asked, still rubbing the sleep from my eyes.

"Come on, Cap, that's Cajun for how's it going. I'm practicing."

"We've created a monster, haven't we?" I said.

"Nah. I'm just always the easy target for kidding from the gang. This time, Jerry pulled the short straw. I like to watch him twitch when I slaughter the French words."

Shaking my head, I said, "Proceed at your own peril there, sailor. I'm here to relieve you."

"Aye, El-Ca-pi-tain. Nothing to report. It's been a quiet watch. We should be on the first set of coordinates in a little over two hours."

"Good. Catch a nap and then check in with Mac. You'll need to get briefed up on the *Sinbad* as soon as you can."

"Read the ops guide last night before turning in. It's an impressive machine. Mac's made a plan for me to put hands on controls at seven this morning."

"Good. What's your first impression of Mac?"

"Seems capable and competent. He's a cool customer, though. All business."

"Noted," I said.

"I'll be on deck at seven," Beau said as he stepped through the hatch.

I turned and checked our position and the readings on the engine gauges as I started my watch. Everything looked in order. About the time I realized a stop in the galley before coming up would've been better, I felt a hand against the small of my back.

"Good morning. I bet this'll help a little." It was Jas, with a mug of coffee.

"Wow, good morning. That's even better than a Rudy breakfast surprise," I said accepting the mug.

"That's good to know," she said as she gave my upper back a subtle rub. "What's our status this morning?"

"We'll be on the first set of coordinates in under two hours, and we'll start our grid search."

"I'll have Woody ready to launch as soon as we identify a target with the main sonar."

"Perfect. Rudy can help Morgan launch," I said.

"Roger that. I'll be in the camera shop if you need me," she said, turning to leave the pilothouse.

I watched her leave for much longer than I normally would have. Even before the first sip of the coffee and caffeine, the warmth of her lying there with me the night before was still warming my chest as I stood there in a predawn daze.

"Whoa, Brother. You still got it bad."

Morgan's words jolted me out of my stupor as I jerked around to face him.

"Would you stop?" I groaned.

"What? Hey, I'm all for it. I just thought you'd been way beyond this part by the time I got back."

"What part is that?" I asked

"Like the part when it took you two months to ask Marilyn Wilson to the prom. That part."

"I really should've left you sleeping in that cargo truck. I could've been loaded and gone. If only I hadn't pulled back that one stinking tarp."

"Yeah, but then you'd miss all this," Morgan said, pointing to himself with his smart-ass knob turned up to eleven.

"Did you sleep, butthead?" I asked.

Morgan laughed. "Wow, you're all 'right out of eleventh grade' this morning, aren't you? But, yes, I did. In fact, my rack never felt so good."

I chuckled with him now. "Good. I know you needed it."

Morgan had a thermos in his hand and he raised it to offer me a warm-up and I lifted my cup for the pour.

"You gonna tell me what happened out there?" I asked.

Morgan's face turned solemn or maybe it was just acceptance, as he shook his head slightly. "Not much to tell, really. By the time the team caught up with Vega and her cronies, they'd hired a team of Sicarios for protection. They'd been hiding for weeks in an old converted grain silo. They were hungry, mean, and desperate."

"I read the news account when the story first broke, but there weren't many details," I said.

"If the whole truth had come out, the Mexican government would've been even more embarrassed than they already were, so there'll never be any more details. Even though the team leader gave them the opportunity to surrender, we knew Vega wouldn't. After four of the Sicarios went down, one of the ex-secretaries managed to crawl out and surrender. I imagine he'll never see daylight again."

"I read there were losses on both sides," I said.

Morgan looked down. "Yeah. One of the agents on our team got hit early in the fight. He was a good guy." Morgan smiled suddenly. "Funny too. He did a great Christopher Walken imitation. He could quote all of Walken's lines from the SNL 'cowbell' skit by heart."

"What about Vega?"

"She was lost in the explosion," Morgan said flatly.

"Explosion?" I asked.

"The explosion that collapsed the twenty-five-foot-high concrete silo she was firing from, into three feet of rubble. Like I said, it's over."

We both sat there quietly, sipping our coffee and finally, I looked up at my brother and asked, "You okay?"

"Yep. But it still doesn't get any easier," he said, staring out of one of the pilothouse windows.

Vega and her mercenaries would have continued to pursue our team and would stop at nothing to recover and suppress the information we'd gathered regarding the missing islands and oil exploration scam. We both knew that.

Morgan would protect his family and our team at all costs. We knew that too. But I hurt knowing my brother had added another event to a list of things that only a warrior has to live with.

"You up for this chase?" I asked.

Morgan's head snapped back to look me straight in the eyes. "Hell yes."

Chapter 8

As THE GOLDEN ORB of the morning sun slipped the watery grip of the Gulf horizon, a pinging alarm from the navigation system chimed, signaling we'd arrived at the coordinates where we'd begin our grid search for the sleeping X-601. Glancing at the video monitor mounted in the helm console, I could see the crew activity on the aft deck. Rudy and Morgan were preparing the hoist that would lift our ROV, Woody, from its cradle and launch when we were ready. On the opposite side of the deck, Beau and Mac Summers scoured and examined every inch of the *Sinbad*, with the intensity of a pair of pollinating bees, checking and reviewing every component and system. I brought the boat to idle speed and picked up the radio and keyed the mic.

"We're at the end of the string. I'm going to push ahead slow and start our sonar scan. Jas, will you monitor the redundant sonar feed from the edit bay? Two sets of eyes are better than one."

"Roger that," Jas called back. "I'm in the bay, ready to go."

"Rudy and Morgan, we'll launch Woody if we mark any targets we think need a closer look."

"Copy that. We'll be ready," Morgan replied.

I began our search track, keeping our speed at five knots across the bottom three hundred twenty feet below our hull. For the first hour, the sonar revealed nothing unusual. The typical bumps, shallow trenches, and an occasional trash pile scrolled across the sonar screen as we progressed along the first lane of the grid I'd inputted into the nav system. I was just settling in for the grind when Morgan's voice came over the radio.

"Hey, Michael, we've got a bogie headed our way off the starboard quarter. It's a little over two miles out, maybe fifty feet off the deck."

"It's the drone I expect," I called back.

"We'll get a good look in about two minutes. I think it'll cross just in front of us."

Who was piloting this drone, and from where? It was troubling enough that a threat of terrorism was this close to

US shores. But the fact that a radical faction was this well funded and had access to this level of hardware was even scarier. I stepped out onto the starboard wing bridge and raised the binoculars. It was the drone all right. But now, speeding across the surface, any laser scanning that might be coming from the drone was invisible in the bright sunlight. Two minutes later, the drone crossed in front of us, sixty yards from our bow and intersecting our course at a forty-five degree angle. I followed the drone with the binoculars as it trailed away. When it was almost out of sight, I saw the dark craft start a long banking turn to the north before settling back onto a course in our general direction.

"Morgan, it's coming back for another pass." There was no reply. "Morgan, you copy?"

Still nothing. The drone was a mile out and closing. "Beau, Rudy, anybody got eyes on Morgan?"

"He said he'd be right back and ran inside," Rudy called over the radio. I pulled out my phone and dialed the commander's number. It rang once.

"Go for Worley," he replied.

"Commander, are you reading the drone on your radar?"

"We are. I can see he's crossing your course. Tell Morgan he has permission to use the Sling-Shot."

"What's the Sling-Shot?" I asked. But before Worley could reply, the answer appeared on deck. Morgan trotted out onto the bow with a strange looking weapon slung under one arm.

"Commander, I'll call you back," I said, ending the call.

The rifle-like weapon was all black with a shoulder stock like a common long-gun. There was a large cube-shaped rectangle protruding down from the trigger area, but it was thicker than a magazine for bullets. The barrel section was a forked set of flat rectangles about two feet long that were spread apart six inches at the far end. *The Sling-Shot, what a great name.* Along the flat side surface of the barrel extensions, there was a row of small green lights that cycled from the body of the weapon outward toward the barrel tips.

The drone was three hundred yards out now. It would cross our bow again at a forty-five degree angle to our course. Morgan shouldered the Sling-Shot and aimed toward the incoming drone. When the bird was fifty yards off our bow, I could see Morgan's hand move as he depressed the trigger. I squinted a little, not sure what to expect from the bizarre looking rifle. Through my squint, it seemed the only sign that the weapon fired was the lights along the barrel that turned from green to blinking red. Two seconds later, the unmanned drone did two corkscrew rolls and dove like a dying bird the remaining fifty feet into the calm waters of the Gulf.

"Well, I'll be damned," Rudy called on the radio.

I pulled back on the throttles, bringing us to idle speed as

I shot back quickly. "Rudy, Beau, Jerry, let's get the RIB launched and see if we can recover that drone."

The crew scrambled into action. Within two minutes, they snapped our twenty-six foot RIB, recently dubbed *Pinto*, into the hoist, ready to lower it over the starboard aft deck rail.

The drone was still floating two hundred yards from our position, but it was floating low in the water. If we couldn't reach it in the next few minutes, it would sink three hundred feet to the bottom. I turned the wheel, steering the boat in the direction of the half-floating drone, closing the distance another fifty yards before shifting the transmission into neutral. I didn't want to crowd the downed aircraft in order to give the RIB crew ample room to work.

"Lowering the RIB," Rudy called over the radio as I watched the *Pinto*, with Beau, Morgan, and Jerry aboard, descend below the aft deck rail on the helm video monitor.

I keyed the mic. "The drone is still on the surface, but it's getting lower every minute. You guys need to hurry."

"We'll be on its position in ninety seconds," Beau called back.

Seconds later, the RIB shot away from the starboard side of the boat on a beeline to the sinking drone's position. The RIB and crew covered half the distance to the drone when a crack and boom rattled the pilothouse. A giant plume of white water erupted from the position where I'd last seen the drone. Morgan banked the RIB into a hard turn, but not before the shockwave threw Jerry from the back of the boat. I hit the master alarm on the helm console, unleashing a wailing siren ship wide that would scramble the remaining crew out on deck. I yelled into the mic, "Man overboard! Man overboard! Prepare to recover from the starboard aft platform." I jammed the shift lever forward into gear to push *Water Horse* closer to the RIB's position. It was way too early in this job to get someone hurt. Morgan yanked the wheel and spun the RIB around alongside Jerry as he treaded water. He was conscious and alert, so that was a good sign. Beau leaned over the starboard tube of the RIB and snatched Jerry out of the drink like he weighed twenty pounds. Even from my position in the pilothouse, I could see that Jerry was bleeding from one ear, but was able to stand unassisted in the cockpit. He even pushed Beau in the chest after what I guessed was a bad Cajun remark.

"Jas, grab the med kit. Jerry looks injured."

"Already have it," she called back.

Morgan maneuvered the RIB against our starboard quarter as Rudy lowered the hoist. After snapping in the lifting rings, the boat and crew rose off the water and over the aft deck. In two minutes, Rudy and Jas had the RIB perched back in its cradle as Beau and Morgan, along with Mac Summers, helped Jerry out of the RIB, guiding him to sit on a nearby crate while Jas assessed his injuries.

"How is he?" I called over the radio.

Morgan answered as he watched Jas finishing her examination. "He's likely ruptured his right eardrum, and he's pissed he fell out of the boat. But other than that, I think our boy is going to be okay."

My shoulders fell a few inches with the relief that no one was seriously injured.

"Pretty clear no one wanted that drone recovered," I called back.

"Seems so," Morgan said.

"I'm going to put us back on the search grid. You got things back there?" I asked.

"I got it, Brother."

It was clear that serious players were intent on finding the X-601. We were in a race and there was no time to waste. Spinning the wheel, I steered *Water Horse* back on course and onto the lane of the search grid and engaged the autopilot. I picked up my phone and redialed Worley's number, which he answered after one ring.

"Worley."

"So, the Sling-Shot is very effective," I said.

Worley laughed. "Let's hear it, Captain."

I gave Worley the blow-by-blow of Morgan's taking

down the drone with the Sling-Shot and its self-destruction before our team could recover it.

"Damn," Worley gruffed. "I wish we could've gotten more information from that drone, but I'm grateful your crew is okay."

"Us too, Commander. We don't like not knowing who we're up against. In fact, I'd like to get another member of our team cleared for security. We have a research badger that's provided intel when conventional sources weren't helpful. If she passes your screening, I'd like to brief her."

"Text me her name and social and I'll run her info."

"Thanks, Commander. If you see anything coming our way, let us know."

"Will do, Captain."

I ended the call and immediately texted Ellie's information to Worley. Our younger sister, Ellie, was an award-winning investigative reporter with a large New York publication. She was an absolute bulldog for uncovering answers to who did what, when they did it, and if they got paid for it. If there was any trace of electronic footprints within the hard to find information, she'd find it. Morgan and I tapped her for intelligence work on many of our assignments. Ellie loved to be neck deep in any stirred pot, so when we called, the answer was always yes. Sometimes after an assignment, she could write about what we discovered and sometimes . . . not.

I dialed our sister's number, and she picked up in less than a full ring.

"Is he home?" she asked without saying hello.

"He is, and he's fine."

She was quiet for several seconds and after a muffled sniffle, her normal uber-confidence was back in force. "Well, I hope you smacked him around a bit."

"I did." I laughed. "He's good, Sis, really."

"Okay, good. Where are you now?"

"In the Gulf," I answered.

"In the Gulf? . . . that's all I get is 'in the Gulf'?"

"We're working, El."

"You're already on a job!" she yelled, then caught herself as it must have registered that she was still in the middle of the newsroom. "You're already on a job?" she repeated, much softer.

"We're in the Gulf, that's all I can say now. I'm trying to get you cleared for a more detailed conversation. Would you be open to that?"

"Does a dog wish he had opposable thumbs? Hell yes, I want in."

"I'll have an answer soon and I'll call you back."

"What can I do in the meantime?" she asked.

"Would you call Mom and Dad and tell them Morgan's home and safe?"

"There'll be hell to pay because he hasn't already called, but I'll do my best 'little sister' cover job."

"He'd appreciate it, I'm sure."

"Oh, it'll cost him, don't worry."

"I have no doubt," I said. "I'll call as soon as your clearance goes through."

"You better," she said, channeling our mom. "If I have to write another 'insider trading' piece this month, I'll run screaming from the building." Then her voice changed into the younger sibling I'd grown up with. "But hey, Michael?"

"Yeah?"

"Be careful, okay? I just got you both back. Let's keep it that way."

"Will do, Sis. Love you."

"Love you both," she said, and I ended the call.

I felt a hand rub my back, and I turned. It was Jas, armed with a thermos, and ready to stand watch.

"El?" she asked.

"Yeah. I've asked Worley if he can clear her, so we can read her in."

"Good idea. I'm here to relieve you."

"How's Jerry?" I asked.

"He's fine. His ear is ringing like hell, but mostly I think he's embarrassed it knocked him out of the boat. It was a hell of a shockwave. I think the windshield blocked most of it from hitting Morgan and Beau."

"I'm glad he's okay," I said.

"Oh yeah, he's good. He'll be ready for his watch in four hours."

"Hey, any thoughts about Mac?"

"Good guy, I think. All business. A little too serious to be considered fun, but this is serious business, so I'll take it."

I nodded. "Anything about his background?"

"Not much. Did a stint with a US Coast Guard MSRT team. Not sure how he ended up assigned to Naval Intelligence."

"Coast Guard MSRT is no joke," I said, absorbing the info on our mini-sub driver. I'd accepted new crew members a little too soon on past assignments and our last client wanted to kill us, so I cut myself some slack for wanting to be extra careful. "We're five miles from making our turn on the next leg of the grid. It's in the nav computer."

"What's that?" Jas asked, pointing to a spec on the horizon.

I'd been on the phone and hadn't seen the target appear on the radar. I grabbed the binoculars for a closer look and was relieved to see it was just a shrimp boat. They were in shallower water and not headed in our direction.

"Shrimper," I said. "Nevertheless, keep an eye out for them."

Jas placed a target marker on the vessel with the joystick on the radar while nodding. "Roger that."

Chapter 9

STEPPING INTO THE GALLEY, I found Jerry sitting at the table, sipping a cup of coffee, and finishing a breakfast burrito. Rudy stood at the stove, shining his special skillet like a surgeon caring for a specialized instrument.

"I put a Rudy burrito in him. He'll be right as rain in no time."

"Always works for me," I said. "How do you feel, Jerry?"

"I'm fine, Cap. Just caught me off guard, that's all. I'll be ready for a helm shift at two."

"How's the ear?"

"Ringing like hell, but I can still hear out of it," he said.

"I want you checked out by the doc when we get back in. Understood?"

"Will do, Cap."

I left Jerry to heal, stomach first, and headed to the aft deck. I wanted to check in with Beau, Morgan, and Mac Summers. Out on deck, Beau and Mac were still going over various aspects of *Sinbad*'s systems as Morgan watched. Mac had Beau in the front cockpit seat, coaching as Beau manipulated two of the four robotic arms attached to the front of the submersible. Four feet from the submersible's front was a twenty-foot length of one-inch-braided line lying on the deck within reach of the robotic arms. Walking up next to Morgan, I asked, "What's that all about?"

"Mac wants him to tie a knot in that line with the grippers on the ends of the arms."

"This should be good," I said.

Through *Sinbad*'s front glass, we watched as Beau twisted the right and left joysticks to control the hydraulic appendages, directing them to reach out and grasp the line with one of the grippers. The mechanical arm movements were jerky as Beau's joystick control seemed to overshoot, then undershoot the distances to the line. Mac continued patiently directing and correcting Beau's hand movements despite our marine's growing sense of frustration. But then, two minutes later, I saw a noticeable change in Beau's face as he nodded along with Mac's instruction. Beau's next try looked like he'd been at the controls for years. Under his control, the arms reached out and with one finger of the grippers, it lifted a section of the line two feet off the deck. The motors of the robotic hands whirred and spun, as the pinchers of the right-hand gripper grasped the line firmly. Another mechanical spin and the arm twisted a loop into the line that dangled below. Now with the other arm, Beau picked up another section of the line and completed a knot that he tightened on itself before dropping it to the deck.

"Fast learner!" Morgan said, as Mac clapped Beau on the shoulder, indicating a good job. Morgan and I gave a few claps of applause, catching Beau's attention.

The upper hatch was still open and we could hear Beau's muffled voice. "We need one of these, Captain!"

"Oh yeah?" I said. "Who's going to pay for it?"

"Only about eight million," Mac added.

"Is that all?" I said, laughing. "My 'under the mattress' fund is a little shy of that."

Mac crawled out of the cockpit and stepped out onto the deck, joining Morgan and me as Beau used the arms to untie his hard-won knot.

"He's a freakishly quick study," Mac said, motioning his head back toward the submersible.

"Yeah, he's proved that on several occasions," Morgan said.

Beau held the now knotless line in the air with the arm and gripper shouting, "Oooh what-a gonna did!"

Morgan and I both shook our heads at Beau's commitment to the Cajun speak.

"Yep, despite all appearances, he's smart and has impressive skills underneath that heavy cloak of jarhead."

"What?" Beau said, dropping the line from the arm's
gripper.

"Nothing. That's good work buddy," I replied, as Beau
resumed mastering *Sinbad*'s controls.

"How about you, Mac?" I said, turning to the submersible
pilot. "I understand you spent some time with a Coast Guard
MSRT team."

"That's right," Mac replied. "I spent a lot of time in the
Caribbean trying to find out how the cartels were using subs
and underwater pick up spots to smuggle their wares into
Miami. The speed at which those bad guys are advancing
their tactics is scary."

"That is scary," I said.

"Where you from originally?" Morgan asked.

"Right here in New Orleans. It's part of the reason Worley reached out and tapped me for this assignment. I'm a
third generation Orleanian. I shrimped these waters with my
grandfather almost as soon as I could walk. My dad didn't
want anything to do with the water and he became a contractor in the area. It must have skipped a generation, because I
could never get enough of the Gulf. Me and Grandad fished

together after school and on weekends until we lost him the summer before I started high school.

"How old was he?" I asked.

"Ninety-three," Mac answered. "He was a tough SOB. I miss him. Anyway, I knew I had to be on the water, so I joined the Coast Guard right out of high school."

"We're glad to have you, Mac. And you've made a thick-necked water dog very happy riding back seat with you," I said, pointing to Beau, grinning like a nine-year-old, as he tied more knots with the motorized arms and hands.

"Bon job, cher!" Mac said to Beau.

"Oh hell, please don't encourage him," Morgan said, as we all laughed.

There's not much to do while running a sonar grid search but try to keep yourself busy while you watched the paint dry. Morning had turned into late afternoon as I made another lap around the main deck, enjoying the weather and thinking. A drone with a scanning laser and self-destruct features was highly advanced equipment. If it was European extremists searching for the sleeping X-601, they were very well financed, and that would make them even more dangerous. I'd made it to the stern and watched as our long, silvery white wake trailed behind our course, stretching toward the horizon. My radio chirped, and Jas called out.

"Cap, just marked a pretty large target. Wanna come take a look?"

"On my way," I said, motioning for Morgan to come along.

Stepping into the pilothouse, I could see the white shaded object on the sonar all the way from the rear door.

"Big target. A little shy of eighty feet, I think," Jas said, pointing to the image on the screen. "There's some other debris nearby, but could be our sub."

"Do we have any specs on the X-601?" Morgan asked.

"Not many. Under a hundred feet long, but not sure how much under," I said. "Let's make another pass across this location and scan it from another angle with the sonar."

"Roger that," Jas said as she turned the wheel, bringing *Water Horse* around for another pass. It was after three in the afternoon and the sun was already low in the February sky as Jas swung our bow to the west and on around onto a course back over the target. The three of us watched the screen intently as we approached the coordinates. There it was again. A long tube-shaped object tapered at one end.

"Only one way to find out," I said. "Let's hold on station and launch Woody."

"On it," Morgan said, leaving the pilothouse.

"I'll relieve you at the helm, go drive Woody," I said, stepping up to the wheel. Jas turned and brushed firmly against me as we traded positions. There was more than enough room for her to step around me, but she didn't.

"The helm is yours," she said, giving me a dangerous smile. "I'll be on coms as soon as we get Woody launched."

"Yeah . . . roger that."

I watched an extra beat as Jas left the pilothouse. She could make a pair of cargo pants and T-shirt look better than should be legal.

Turning back to the helm, I engaged the "hover" option on the autopilot controls. The system would use our GPS position, then take control of the main engine's transmission in conjunction with *Water Horse*'s thrusters to hold us on this exact location. From the monitor displaying the aft deck camera, I could see Morgan as he lifted Woody up and over the stern rail with the boom arm. Our ROV lowered out of sight below the stern rail, followed by Morgan's voice over the radio.

"Woody's wet," he called.

"I have telemetry and control," Jas followed.

I hit the selector switch on my helm monitor and the display changed to a split screen of Woody's main camera and the new HIC-SA sonar image. At this distance from shore, the water was exceptionally clear and the camera's image was perfect. But as the ROV went deeper, the added clarity of the sonar would prove helpful. Woody pitched downward and began the descent three hundred feet to the bottom. There wasn't much to see on the trip down, but at the eighty-foot mark, Woody's external lights switched on, illuminating the particulates, small jellyfish, and other organisms teaming in the ocean water. Eight minutes into the ROV's descent, on the monitor, I could make out the darker bottom approaching as the ROV leveled out at search depth. As Woody moved forward to the north, scanning across the seafloor, debris appeared on the bottom.

"You seeing this?" Jas called to me over the radio.

"I am," I answered. "Hard to make out anything."

Marine growth covered the unidentifiable objects on the sandy bottom, but it was apparent they weren't naturally occurring. Forward of the ROV's course and out of the reach of the onboard lights, the new sonar pierced the darkness, giving us a glimpse of what lay ahead. The HIC-SA display began outlining the tubular shape that we initially spotted on the main sonar. Moments later, the lights and camera caught up and a larger section of wreckage slowly emerged into the frame. Even though a heavy layer of living growth and small corals covered the large object, it was clear to see it was a hull of some kind.

"Maybe the subchaser actually sunk the 601 in 1944," I said over the radio.

"Ha! We're never that lucky," Morgan answered as he

watched the feed from the edit bay with Jas. "In fact, look at that," he said as Jas brought Woody to a stop over a small section of the hull that was strangely not covered in growth. As the ROV got within a few feet of the surface of the object, I could see it.

"That looks like an aluminum skin, doesn't it?" I said.

"This may be an old B-17," Morgan said. "The size is right."

"Check the sonar," Jas called. "Those could be the wings."

Two other targets, detached from the primary hull, appeared on the sonar, roughly perpendicular to the hull shape, as Woody progressed along the object.

"A few 17s went down in the Gulf. Mostly during training," Morgan said.

Woody continued to creep slowly forward until it reached the end of the hull shape when something caught my eye.

"Jas, spin and drop down on the east side of the nose there."

"Spinning," Jas answered.

As the ROV dropped down, the camera revealed a cleaner section of the nose. Woody's exterior lights lit up an exciting surprise that confirmed Morgan's guess. Looking back at the camera over a demure bare shoulder stood a cartooned bathing beauty with her title painted in bright red script: "Li'l Nell."

"Whoa," Jas said. "She's beautiful."

"The B-17 changed the course of the war. They were incredible aircraft," Morgan said.

A chime rang on the helm station, interrupting our surprise find. I looked up from the monitor to see it was the alarm I set on the radar, to alert us if a target crossed inside the three-mile perimeter I set up earlier. It was twilight and would be fully dark in another twenty minutes. I grabbed the binoculars and scanned the horizon to the west. I couldn't see any running lights, but there was still enough light in the western sky to reveal the outline of a boat headed our way.

"What's the alarm?" Jas called.

"There's a boat headed our way, with no running lights," I answered before taking another look to confirm a sickening suspicion. "I think it's the shrimper we saw earlier. Jas, put Woody into emergency recovery mode and let's get everyone ready."

I reached under the front edge of the nav console and engaged a switch that changed all the interior lights throughout the entire ship to red. There was no alarm, but the change that occurred only to the interior sections of the ship would initiate a rehearsed set of actions from our crew. A nasty group of mercenaries boarded the *Water Horse* on our last assignment and the silent red light alarm was one of the many procedure updates we'd made to our readiness during our downtime over the holidays in the Keys.

Kneeling on the floor of the pilothouse, under the overhang of the nav station, I pressed down on a section of the teak and holly flooring that sprang up with a click. Raising the section of flooring triggered dim LED lights that illuminated the hidden compartment. From inside the floor locker, I removed a Heckler & Koch HK416 rifle, two extra mags, tactical Kevlar vest, a single ear com set, and a Springfield armory 9mm with an appendix holster. I slipped the vest over my head and secured the side straps. Then I secured the holstered pistol inside my waistband and checked the mag on the 416. I grabbed an old sweatshirt I'd left in the pilothouse and pulled it on over the vest. Ship wide, the new silent alert initiated similar gearing up from the rest of the crew. Morgan stepped into the pilothouse carrying a matching HK416 as I replaced the floor section over the covert locker with a spring-loaded click.

"How far out?" Morgan asked.

"Two miles now," I answered. "It's a shrimper. Hell, his lights could just be out. They're not exactly known for running ultra-maintained boats." But as the words left my mouth, they sounded even less convincing.

"Like I said before—"

"Yeah, I know. We're never that lucky," I said. "Has Mac been briefed?" I asked.

"Yes, Beau briefed Mac and me on the new emergency procedures as soon as we left the terminal. I like the red lights. Good thinking, Brother."

"I thought you might. I'm sure you can tighten things up, but we were muddling along without you."

"You've never muddled along at anything. The new hidden gear lockers are perfect. I passed Mac on my way up, pulling a Mossberg from the new hidden aft deck locker. I'm going back below to see if everyone else is set."

Touching my right ear, I engaged the mic on the new bone induction com set and said, "Com check."

Rudy was the first to answer. "Rudy's up with Harper. We're five by five, Cap."

"Beau ready. Just inside the aft port side hatch."

"Jas is on. Inside the forward main deck hatch, port."

"Jerry. Five by five on the pilothouse roof. I have eyes on."

Jerry would be equipped with a Mk12 SPR rifle with night optics.

"They're less than a mile out," I said over the coms.

"They're running dark ship wide. Five crew visible. No weapons that I can see. They look like typical shrimpers," Jerry called.

"Morgan, you read that?" I said.

"Got ya. I'm behind the large gear locker on the aft deck," Morgan answered.

"Mac, you read?" I called.

"Go for Mac. I'm with Beau."

"All right everyone, hold tight. This may be nothing at all," I said to the crew.

When the shrimp boat was seventy-five yards out, it slowed to idle speed off our port side and turned broadside to us. As the boat drifted to a stop, a man exited the pilothouse out onto the shrimper's starboard deck.

"Ahoy! *Water Horse*."

I leaned the rifle on the inside of the hatch before stepping out onto the port side wing deck. It was dark, but there was enough starlight for me to have a dim view of the man. The shrimper looked to be in his thirties, lean and unshaven. He wore a pair of black oiler bottoms with the suspenders pulled up over a dirty undershirt. The other men on board remained just inside the shadows.

"What seems to be the problem?" I yelled.

"We lost our genny. Got no 'lectrics and we can't make ice for our catch. If we have to go in, there's no way to make a quota in time to get paid. We thought you boys might have a mechanic on board."

His looks were right, and he sure sounded like many of the watermen I've met over the years. But the hair on the back of my neck refused to relax.

"Our engineer's injured. Got a bum arm, sorry. I'd be glad to make a call and get somebody sent out for you."

"Aw come on, Captain, you gotta have another swab on that big, pretty boat that can turn a wrench."

"Sorry, Captain, we're mostly scientists and cameramen here."

"Well, damn. I hate to hear that, Captain."

"Why's that?" I yelled back.

The burst came from somewhere on the work deck of the shrimp boat. I had a sense of something hitting the hatch frame to my left one split second before a rhino hit me on the left side of my chest, knocking me off my feet back into the pilothouse and flat on my back. I heard the thud of my back against the floor, then the BOOM of a rifle shot.

Chapter 10

IT FELT LIKE MY EYES were just closed for a few seconds, but when I opened them, Jas was leaning over me.

"Michael. Hey, Michael, you're okay. You were hit in the vest."

I tried to sit up, but I only made it a few inches off the floor before the knife-like pain shot through my ribs, blurring my vision. Jas put her hand on my chest, urging me back down.

"Whoa. Let's just stay here and catch your breath for a minute?"

"The crew okay?" I asked through closed eyes.

"Everyone is fine. Jerry took out the shooter, and Rudy put a football sized hole through the shrimp boat deckhouse six inches from the captain's head and the rest of their crew surrendered as soon as they realized they were outgunned."

I exhaled, relieved at the news. "Who are they?" I asked.

"We don't know yet. Morgan and Beau are securing the boat and crew."

I was feeling stronger and more together, and was ready to try and move. "Help me sit up," I grunted.

Jas hooked one hand in the front of my vest and one on my shoulder and together we started upward. It hurt but was manageable.

"How's it feel?" Jas asked.

"Like someone hit me with a ball bat on the left side of my chest." During training sessions, I'd tried to imagine how it'd feel to get shot. Morgan's descriptions of the gunshots he'd survived did little to prepare me for the impact of the experience.

Jas dug into a small tear on the left side of my vest and pulled out the 9mm round that was just inside the first few layers of Kevlar.

"Be grateful for the vest. Any trouble breathing?"

"No. Just sore."

"You probably cracked a few ribs."

Morgan stepped into the pilothouse, winded from rushing up the steps.

"How is he?" he asked, before even recognizing I was sitting up.

"I'm fine," I said.

Morgan knelt down, checking the tear in my vest. "You sure you're good?" he asked with a worried look I rarely saw from my brother.

"I'm good. But it feels like a car hit me."

Morgan chuckled. "It's supposed to, Brother. It reminds you to not get shot again."

"Message received," I said, trying to move my arms and legs more to see what else hurt.

"I'm going to take him below and tape up his ribs," Jas said.

"Want me to pull Jerry off overwatch to check him over?" Morgan asked.

Jerry was a paramedic before joining us and served as our field medic. But he'd done a good job cross training us in case of any onboard emergencies.

"If it's more than bruising, I'll get Jerry. Until then, I like knowing he's up top looking out for us," Jas said

"After getting taped up, think you'll feel like stepping next door to see if we can get some answers?" Morgan asked.

"Hell yes," I said, shifting to get my feet under me to stand.

"Easy," Jas urged as she helped me up.

"I'm good. Tape me up and then I definitely have some questions for our shrimpers."

"No rush, they'll keep," Morgan said. "Beau, Mac, and Harper are standing watch on the working deck with the four remaining crew cuffed and quiet."

"Give me ten and I'll be good to go," I said, as Jas and I made our way down to my cabin.

I eased down on the end of my bed. My side ached, but the shakiness in my knees was subsiding. Jas helped me pull the straps of the tactical vest off and up over my head. If I had any doubt of the effectiveness of the vest before, I didn't now. It had made the difference between being here or not. She helped me pull off my T-shirt, trying not to make me move my arms too much. A deep bruise was already forming at the base of my left peck. Jas looked closer and gently put her hand against my bruised ribs. Despite the pain, her touch was like a warming balm against the impact point on my side. She held her hand there against me and looked up to meet my eyes.

"Let's not do that again, okay? You really scared me, Michael."

Putting my right hand on top of hers, I met her concerned look. "I understand."

We'd had a close call on our last assignment when Jas was almost pulled into a collapsing sinkhole on the bottom of the Gulf. The thoughts of Jas being hurt or lost had shaken me in a way that I was still struggling with. Jas leaned forward and kissed me gently on the lips, lingering there as I inhaled the hints of vanilla and spice that followed her everywhere. As she slowly pulled away, she met my gaze again with her deep emerald-green eyes.

"Let's get you taped up and go rattle some cages next door."

I opened my mouth to speak, but Jas just put her fingertips on my lips.

"Now raise your arms just a little," she instructed, more serious now. She pulled a roll of self-adhesive gauze out of the med kit and started wrapping it around my upper torso. She followed that with some tape.

"I'm going to wrap this pretty tight. Are you ready?"

"I am," I answered, but still winced as the first tight wrap of the tape put pressure on my chest. I'd be sore as hell for a while, but the pressure of the wrap helped. All finished, Jas helped me with my shirt and extended her hand to help me up. With a pull, I stood and surprised her by pulling her against me.

"Now I know why the guys like you to doctor them instead of Jerry."

She pulled away and poked the heavily bruised area through my bandages.

"Oww," I gasped. Then I pulled her against me again and returned her kiss. "Thank you."

Out on deck, the crew had tied the shrimp boat along our

port side. The vessel looked to be eighty feet, and according to the painted name on her bow, was christened the *Mudbug*. It was obvious now, the shrimpers had been playing possum, because one of our crew found the breakers to the working deck lights of the shrimp boat, and now they not only lit up the entire fishing vessel, but also the port side of *Water Horse*. Morgan met us on deck.

"You good?"

"Don't make me laugh and I'll be fine. How's Jerry?" I asked.

"He's good. Doesn't like it, but he knows the guy left him no choice. He'll be fine."

"Did we recover Woody?" I asked.

"We did. Sitting back in his cradle, hooked to the boom, ready to go."

Rudy stepped up and around Morgan, still carrying his Mossberg.

"Glad to see you moving around, Cap."

"I heard you added some ventilation to our friend's wheelhouse," I said.

"Jack-wagons thought they were going frog-giggin, but ended up wrestling a few gators."

"Roger that, buddy. Glad you guys had my back."

"Always, Michael," he said, patting me on the shoulder before disappearing into the aft cabin.

Morgan stepped up beside me. "I called Worley, and he's sending an undercover boat out to tow this tub in and take custody of the crew. His team will be here in an hour, but let's see what we can find out before they get here."

"Let's go," I said.

The crew had placed a gangway over to the shrimp boat, so boarding would be easier.

Crossing over onto the aft deck of the shrimper, Beau and Mac stood guard over four men sitting on the deck with their hands bound with zip cuffs. Harper stood nearby with the side of his lip slightly raised, showing a few impressive teeth. On the far side of the deck, a body lay covered with a blanket. I approached the unshaven man that spoke to me from outside the wheelhouse.

"Any reason you felt the need to fire on us, Captain?" I asked.

Now only a few feet from the man, I could see he had very defined features underneath the scruff. His English was perfect, and the Cajun drawl had vanished.

"In every battle, someone must draw first blood," the man said, smiling.

"Hell, Captain, I didn't know we were in a battle," I said.

"This battle has been smoldering for eighty years while you and your weak nation were sleepwalking."

"That sounds just like something I'd expect from radical Eurotrash," Morgan said.

One crewman sprang to his feet, charging toward Morgan. Mac took two steps forward and cracked the man in the chin with the butt of his shotgun, knocking him flat on his back. Harper closed the distance and gave a teeth-bared feral growl at the man. Mac racked a shell into the chamber, pointing the weapon at the man's head. "We have more blankets. Would you like to lie over there next to your friend?"

The man spit out some blood but remained silent as Beau drug him by his collar back in line with the other seated crewmates while the captain maintained his defiant glare at me accompanied with a knowing smile.

"Harper, come," Morgan said, and with his hair still raised along his backbone, Harper came and sat at Morgan's side, but the low growl continued.

"Should we expect more of your fellow shrimpers?" I asked

"We are many. And we are everywhere," he said.

"Ominous," Morgan said.

"I suppose you have nothing to say that might save innocent lives in all this?" I asked.

"No one is innocent, and blood must be shed for the phoenix to rise," he said, grinning.

Like an unexpected agitation of an electric shock, a growing rage roiled in my gut and my ears began to ring. There were so many sick ideologies that the only way for them to advance or grow was through the needless suffering of others. The Nazis killed six million Jews and thousands of American and British citizens eighty years ago. Now, a group of reinvented radicals wanted to try that again? I could decrease that group by one, right here, right now, and unconsciously, my hand reached for my SIG in my waist holster. Morgan stepped behind me and placed a hand on my shoulder, and said to the group, "Anyone else want to help themselves out before your ride to an undisclosed dark-site prison shows up?"

The only response was silence. "Roger that. Black sites coming up," Morgan said, patting me on the back. My gun hand relaxed and dropped to my side.

"You'll want to take a look down there," Beau said, pointing to the large hatch that was in the center of the aft deck.

Morgan walked over and lifted one edge of the hatch and found it equipped with a hydraulic lift. With little effort, the hatch raised to its full, open position as I walked up behind Morgan looking over his shoulder. Lights blinked into life, replacing the darkness in the large space below. The entire hold, designed to store a day's catch, instead contained rows of metal shelves stocked with jerry cans of fuel and other supplies. A metal ladder descended into the space, and Morgan spun to start down the ladder.

"I'll do this. You can stay here," he said.

"Will you shut up and go on? I'm fine," I said.

Morgan smiled and started down. I followed, although a little slower, down the ladder. My left ribs protested, but Jas's tape job made the pain manageable. Once on the floor, a glance deeper into the brightly lit cargo space revealed even more menace. On the bulkheads of the space were charts of the Gulf and the Mississippi River delta along with schematics of what I assumed was the mysterious X-601 boat. Immediately to one side of the line drawings of the boat was an eight-by-ten black-and-white photo of a German sea captain. He stood on a military wharf in his wool double-breasted uniform jacket. Pinned to his uniform was the Iron Cross first-class medal and the U-boat war badge awarded to commanders with at least two wartime sea deployments. There was no name on the photo, but this was undoubtably Hans Schreiber, captain of the X-601. He wasn't smiling in the photo, but his eyes were bright and determined. I wondered if, on the day the picture was taken, he knew he was about to seal the hatch to his boat and likely never see the sun again. What kind of resolve did it take to step forward for a mission like that?

Morgan surveyed and dug through the shelves behind me

while I stood transfixed at the aged photo, of the old sub-mariner. Something dug at me as I stood there trying to get inside the mind of the ghost that stared back at me.

"If you were going to resurrect an old sub, it's what I'd bring," Morgan said as he zig-zagged his way through the aisles of shelving.

"What ya got?" I said over my shoulder, snapping out of my daze.

"In addition to the fuel, we've got lead-acid batteries, a 50mm gun, some food-stuffs and, oh yeah, four shoulder-mounted rocket launchers."

"I guess those are in case the deck-mounted rockets are too old to fire," I said.

"Deck-mounted rockets?" Morgan asked, walking up behind me as I continued to survey the line drawing of the deadly sub. I pointed to the schematic depicting the deck area of the U-boat. I couldn't read the faded German text, but the diagram left no doubt what the launching structures were.

"Whoa," Morgan said, looking closer.

"Can you read any of that?" I asked.

"Not well." He pointed to one section of the text. "But this says, 'extended range V-2 MKII.'"

"It's amazing," I said. This design looks like something from the eighties, not something designed in the forties."

"With just a few twists of fate during the war, it could have been a very different world today," Morgan said. "The Nazis had so many brilliant engineers. Why do you think we recruited so many Germans into our space program? Who's that guy?" Morgan said, pointing to the photograph of the captain.

"I think that's Hans Schreiber, captain of the 601."

"All-business-looking SOB, huh?"

"Just what I was thinking," I answered. "Do you really think the boat could be operational after all these years?"

"I don't know, but these guys certainly think it can, so we need to find it fast," Morgan answered. "But listen," he said, turning to face me. "These guys are true believers. They're not motivated by money or greed, like the last few crazies we've faced. It's a sick, twisted ideology that gets embedded deep into their psyche and it makes them far more dangerous than the worst mercenaries. The crazier they get, the more in control of our emotions we must be. Follow me?"

I let Morgan's words sink in, recalling the rage that almost triggered an unconscious reaction earlier on deck. "Understood."

"But make no mistake. We will end them. But think surgeon removing a cancer, instead of just blowing up the whole building," Morgan added.

"Roger that," I said. "Let's get back on the search. I'm going to have Jas photograph this hold before Worley's team gets here."

"Good thinking," Morgan said, looking at his watch. "They'll be here anytime."

We both took one last glance around the space before Morgan urged me up the ladder.

Back on deck, I motioned for Jas to step over. "Let's grab some stills and video of that compartment before Worley's team shows up."

"Done," she said, before bolting back across the gangway and into the camera shop. She was back in under a minute, camera in hand, and sliding down the ladder into the cargo hold, getting to work. Morgan stepped by me on his way back to our boat with one of the shoulder-mounted rocket launchers slung under his arm.

"What are you doing with that?" I asked.

"May come in handy," he answered with a grin.

"Boat approaching," Beau said, pointing to the northeast horizon.

I touched my ear, engaging the com set I'd almost forgot I was wearing. "Jerry, you got ears?"

"Go for Jerry," he answered immediately.

"You have eyes on the approaching target?"

"Roger. Looks like a pilot boat."

"That's Worley's boys," Morgan said. "The commander said that's what he'd be sending."

I spoke, automatically opening my mic. "Water Horse. Friendly boat approaching, but until that's absolutely confirmed, the red light is on. Team, confirm?"

The "confirm" replies rang through one by one as the pilot boat continued its approach.

Jerry came across our coms. "The pilot boat just called in on the VHF. The captain said, 'codeword: mudbug.'"

Morgan nodded and answered back. "That's our boys, for sure," he said. "Tell them to come alongside the shrimp boat."

"Roger that. I'll tell 'em," Jerry answered.

I stepped over to the cargo hatch. "Jas, boat approaching, so finish up."

"Two minutes," she called back.

I didn't know if Naval Intelligence would want us photographing anything, but I'd already decided we would ask for forgiveness instead of permission.

The pilot boat closed on our position as Jas emerged from the hold. She gave me a nod.

"Got it. I'll get the images and footage on the server."

"Good work," I said, as she crossed back over to our deck.

Three minutes later, the pilot boat pulled alongside. Six large, plain-clothes operators piled out of the cabin, securing the boat before handily relieving Beau and Mac from guard duty.

"We've got quite a suite of luxurious accommodations waiting for these lucky winners," one of the large operators said, unholstering his service weapon to cover the two men sitting closest to him.

I pointed to the captain. "The one in oilers there is the alpha," I said to the man I assumed was the team leader.

"Oh, good!" said the six-three, two-sixty-plus man, wearing a sweatshirt with the sleeves cut off and biceps as big as my thigh.

"We like the alpha dogs. Once neutered, they become surprisingly compliant," the super-sized operator said with a wry grin.

I wasn't the one leaving with this six-man escort team, but the man's words still sent a chill down my spine. I motioned to Morgan nearby. "I'll wrap up here. Will you get the crew ready to get back on the search?"

"Roger that," he said, as he signaled Beau to join him back aboard *Water Horse* with Harper bringing up the rear.

The senior operator approached, extending his hand to me.

"You the captain of that beautiful boat?"

"Guilty," I answered, while shaking hands. "Michael Gannon."

"You can call me Bob," he said with a bad sell job of his assumed name. "Nice looking vessel. And good job bagging this trash. We'll be glad to take them off your hands."

"Please," I said. "We've got a sub to find."

To my surprise, Commander Worley emerged from the cabin of the pilot boat and stepped over onto the shrimp boat deck. "Didn't expect to see you out here," I said.

"Wanted to see this for myself," the seasoned navy man said.

"The interesting stuff is in the hold, down that hatch," I said, pointing to the open access entrance.

Worley made his way down the access ladder and I stayed on deck, letting him explore on his own. The operators transferred the shrimp boat crew over onto the pilot boat and secured them below. "Bob" reemerged from the cabin and stepped back across and approached me.

"Was that your brother on deck?"

"Yeah, why?"

"Morgan Gannon?" he asked.

I chuckled a little. "Yep."

Bob smiled, pulling his ball cap back, scratching his head. "Shit man, these guys picked the wrong boat to pull some pirate stunt."

I unconsciously rubbed the bruised area of my chest through the tight binding of the tape.

"Yeah, and you didn't even meet our engineer."

Bob gave a respectful nod of his head, as Worley emerged from the cargo hold with an ashen expression.

"We gotta find this sub, Captain. How long till you can get back on the search?" he asked me.

"Get this scow off my port side, and we're off," I said.

"Good work here, Michael," he said as he motioned a hand in the air, sending the operators into action, singling up lines and rigging a towline on the bow of the shrimper. "Eleanor passed clearance," Worley called to me over the action on deck. "We need all the intel we can get, so put her to work."

"She'll be my next call, Commander. I'm sure she won't disappoint."

Chapter 11

I STOOD ON OUR PORT SIDE DECK and watched as the pilot boat put the shrimper in tow and headed northeast back toward Worley's terminal. It was well after midnight, and the absence of the shrimp boat's deck lights left us in the Gulf's darkness. In my encounter with the leader of the radicals, the line "we are everywhere" left me uneasy. They appeared as typical as any watermen I'd run across in all my years on and around boats. When I thought of all the back water harbors, basins, and docks on the panhandle of the Gulf, more of them could be anywhere and everywhere. Working boats, shrimpers, and fishermen were as common as seagulls on this body of water and largely ignored by everyone. As Worley's team towing the shrimper became a small spec on the horizon, the realization that a nice complement of reinforcements, just left us alone in the Gulf. But, we'd have to worry about that later. I called out on my coms. "Jerry, can you come down and get us underway and back on the search grid?"

"On my way, Cap. I'll have us scanning in three minutes."

"Excellent," I answered, then turned to head for my cabin.

I eased down into my chair as the remaining drips of adrenaline leaked from my pores. The pain and ache replaced the missing endorphins quickly. Pulling my phone from my cargo pocket, I dialed Ellie. She answered on the second ring.

"Well, am I approved?"

"You are. And hello."

"Yeah, hi. What's first?" she asked, getting right to business.

I gave Ellie as much of the info along with names and events that I could remember from my earlier briefing with Commander Worley, with a promise to upload all the material to a secure link as soon as we were off the phone. I tried to recall the exact words the radical leader used concerning the "rise of the phoenix." That phrase was the most troubling, and I hoped there'd be dark web chatter around that phrase. I could hear Ellie typing furiously as she recorded notes.

"And you promise you're okay?" she asked as the typing stopped.

"I am," I answered. "Oh, and will you pull some background on another name?"

"Shoot," she said.

"See what you can find on a Mac Summers, formerly with Coast Guard MSRT."

"Is he part of your team?"

"He is. Seems like a great guy and he's performed well so far. He's not family, so I'm being ultra cautious."

"Will do," Ellie said. "Give me a few hours and I'll get back with you."

"Great. And thanks, Sis."

"You kidding me? This is way more fun than financial crime!"

"Glad we can help. Love you," I said and ended the call.

My cabin door swung inward without a knock, like being opened by a doctor on rounds. Jas strode purposely inside and stopped in front of me.

"Three hours of rack time, Captain," she said, pointing to my bed.

"But we're back on the grid, we have to—"

"And you're no good to us half-baked. I'll come get you if we hit a target. Just a few hours, yeah?"

I wasn't in much shape to protest, so I stood and crossed the cabin, easing down onto the bed. I had to admit, it felt good. And if I lay very still, nothing hurt. Jas sat down on the edge of the bed next to me and reached to take my hand.

"When this one is over, I think we should talk about this," she said, as she gripped my hand a little firmer.

"We probably should," I said.

"Does that scare you?" she asked.

"Scare? No. Maybe a little nervous it might get weird."

"Because you're my boss?"

"Maybe. And because of what happened with your diving coach," I said.

"Wow, this boat just got a lot smaller."

"The crew looks after you like a little sister. Hard to keep a secret here," I said, smiling.

"You nervous?"

"A little," she answered. "We've got such a good thing here with the whole team."

"Yeah, we do," I said. "But if you keep kissing me, what's a sailor to do?"

She poked me in the ribs again, causing me to flinch at the electric jolt of pain that fired down my left side.

"You are not speeding my healing," I said through a clenched jaw.

"I haven't even begun to speed your healing, sailor," she said with a grin. "I'll come get you in a few hours or the minute we hit a target. Okay?"

"Roger that," I said.

Jas put my hand back on my chest and left me to rest. Shifting slightly on the bed, my ribs reminded me to be still. Lying there in the quiet, the thoughts of having a conversation about my relationship with Jas and the anticipation of finding the sub, had me convinced I'd never fall asleep.

The foot of my bed shook, rattling me conscious.

"Yo! Wake up, swab."

I sat bolt upright, instantly regretting it, as I grabbed my left ribs. "Damn, that hurts," I said. "We hit on something?"

"We did," Morgan said. "You done resting?"

"Your bedside manner sucks. You know that?" I said, swinging my legs over the edge of the bed and standing up.

"I'll bring you a doughnut next time," he said. "You good to go?"

"Yep," I said, cranking a Water Horse ball cap over my bedhead. "You launching the ROV?"

"As soon as you can drag your lame self to the pilot-house," Morgan said.

"The love . . . it just oozes off you, doesn't it?"

"It's a gift."

It was just before five in the morning when I stepped up behind Jerry at the helm, getting my first glance at the sonar image that caused him to put the boat in hover mode. Everything about the target looked like a sleeping sub sitting on the bottom at three hundred fifteen feet.

"What do ya think, Cap?" Jerry asked.

"Certainly looks like it could be our boat," I said. I picked up a radio and called Morgan. "Let's launch Woody."

"Splashing him now," he called back.

"I'm going to step down in the edit bay and observe from there," I said. "You good here, Jerry?"

"Go," he said. "I got this."

I rushed down to the edit bay to find Jas at the controls of the ROV viewing the action on our massive monitor displays set up with the HIC-SA sonar image and the video feed from Woody's forward camera, split-screened across the monitors. The on-screen telemetry from the remote vehicle showed its depth at eighty feet and descending fast. At one hundred fifty feet, the HIC-SA display showed the bottom approaching, but the onboard camera was still just displaying black. Jas hadn't powered up the ROV's lights because there wasn't much to see on the trip down. Six minutes later, the sonar showed a clear image of the bottom terrain as Woody leveled off at three hundred feet, approximately ten feet off the bottom.

"Let's run on the HIC-SA alone for the first part of the search. It's giving us great pictures," Jas said, as she began moving Woody forward toward the target coordinates we'd pinpointed on the ship's main sonar.

"You're driving," I said.

A knock came against the hatch frame of the edit bay and Mac peeked his head in.

"You guys mind if I watch from in here?"

"No, come on in, Mac. Have a seat," I said, motioning for him to join us.

"The pilothouse was getting crowded," he said, dropping into one of the leather easy chairs behind us.

The high resolution sonar clarity was impressive. Even though it was only stark shades of black and white, I couldn't believe the images that filled half of our displays weren't being generated by a camera. As we closed to within one hundred feet of the target, a shallow furrow appeared on the bottom and extended out in front of Woody's course like a trail leading to something large.

"That seems promising," Mac said.

I exchanged looks with Jas before saying, "Ahead slow."

"This is unbelievable," she said, as she gently nudged the right joystick forward, easing the ROV along the long depression in the seafloor. The HIC-SA suddenly lit up with added reflections as we approached something much larger, straight ahead. Jas pushed Woody a few yards closer and stopped in a hover.

"That looks like a pair of propellers to me," she said.

Mac and I stared blankly at the sonar image in front of us. I knew what we were looking for and the images from the main ship's sonar made us sure we'd find it. But sitting here looking at the stark white sonar image of a pair of three blade propellors, from an eighty-year-old boat that virtually no one knew even existed, was still sobering.

"Power up the lights," I said.

Jas flipped a toggle switch on her ROV controls and the camera side of the display brightened to life.

The camera image wasn't any clearer than the sonar, but it added shadow, color, and texture that brought the discovery to life in a whole new way.

"Lying here asleep this whole time," Mac murmured softly.

"Props look intact," Jas said.

"Unbelievable," I said, a little dumbfounded.

The radio sprang to life as Morgan, Jerry, and Rudy watched from the pilothouse.

"Well, this one's not a plane," Morgan called, over the other excited voices watching the images on the helm monitors.

"No. No mistaking what this is," I answered.

There was marine growth on the aft end of the sub for sure, but nothing like what you'd expect to see on a steel structure after this many years on the bottom of the Gulf.

"Let's ease down the starboard side," I said, as Jas spun the ROV slightly before crabbing forward twenty-five feet from the side of the sub's starboard hull.

Jas made some adjustments to the HIC-SA to widen the scan, allowing us to get a better idea of the size of the entire hull.

"Looks like she's about ninety feet long," Jas said, looking at the overlay scale on the screen.

The 601 was sitting perfectly upright on the bottom, with maybe six feet of the hull buried in the sand and mud. Everything about the posture of the boats grounding here on the bottom resembled a careful parking job as opposed to a disabled sub. Mossy growth covered a good portion of the hulking structure, but large patches of steel and rivets were still visible along the topsides of the slumbering war machine. The camera of the slowly moving ROV maneuvered along the hull, unveiling more of the well-preserved boat as we all sat in silence. I sucked in a breath and held it, as the camera zoomed out slightly to reveal the conning tower of the sub, standing defiantly, with its sail observation tower pointing toward the surface. Mac stood, unable to keep his seat as the excitement built as each section of the antique sub came into view on the large screen. I couldn't blame him. The scene playing out on the monitors was hard to believe and I think we were all ramped up as each new section of the sub came into view.

"What's that?" I asked, pointing to an upper section of the conning tower.

Jas slowed the ROV's speed and drifted upward. Woody's lights illuminated the front of the conning tower and she slowed Woody to a stop as the camera centered on what had caught my eye. No one made a sound as we each gawked at the hand-painted artwork, standing vigil over the watery graves of an unknown number of German sailors. The imposing head of a gray-and-black wolf, outlined in blood red, snarled as it peered out into the depths with a squinted red eye. Its neck held a spiked collar with a silver German Iron Cross medallion hanging under the vicious-looking jaws. The muscles in my shoulders tightened as my mind played out the wolf's original mission eighty years ago. A rocket attack launched from the Mississippi River into the US mainland would immediately kill unknown scores of people, but the ensuing national panic would magnify the loss many times over. Morgan's words from earlier came back to me. This was not a plan devised from greed. It was a plan to inflict only two things: pain and loss, conceived by the sadistic group-think of true believers.

Chapter 12

WE WERE GOING TO HAVE TO SHAKE OFF the shock quick and get to work. If we were to believe information from the crew of the resupply boat, we were racing an unknown number of radicals hell-bent on finding the 601 and getting her off the bottom.

"Let's scan the rest of the hull and get *Sinbad* in the water." I turned to face Mac and simultaneously keyed the radio mic. "Beau, you two ready to get wet?" I asked.

"Thought you'd never ask," Mac said and spun, heading to the aft deck.

"On my way," Beau answered.

"Rudy? Will you and Morgan splash our boys?" I called.

"Rigging as we speak," Rudy answered.

"Michael," Jas called, bringing my attention back to the monitors. "Check that out," she said as the ROV maneuvered forward toward the bow on the sub's starboard side.

Ten feet forward of the conning tower, a single circular hatch on the main deck stood sprung open. It looked to be six feet across, almost like a miniature missel silo on a modern day sub. Jas tilted the ROV at a downward angle to peer inside the hatch, and although it was hard to tell for sure, it looked enclosed as if watertight.

"Maybe a radio buoy or an early torpedo counter measure," I guessed aloud.

"Everything about this sub is completely unknown. It could be anything," Jas said.

As the ROV glided further forward toward the sub's bow, the launching structures of the V-2 rockets came into view. Marine growth covered them, yet they appeared surprisingly intact.

"Think those would actually still fire?" Jas asked.

"Don't know, but I bet someone was going to try. Let's make a run down the port side while they're prepping the submersible."

"Down the port side we go," Jas said, as she steered Woody around the nose of the bow before starting aft.

The pass down the port side of the sub revealed no surprises until we were aft of the conning tower. There, ten feet aft of the sail, was an important piece of this puzzle. A raised circular hatch ring positioned on the centerline of the main deck. It had to be the docking collar mentioned in the intel brief. Growth covered the raised steel flange that stood proud of the deck level, but its intended use was clear.

"Let's grab a series of pictures and measurements of that hatch and get them to Worley right away," I said.

"Think *Sinbad* can dock with it?" Jas asked.

"I hope so."

Jas positioned Woody at multiple angles around the docking collar, snapping photos and video with dimensional scale data overlays on the screen. After gathering the pictures, she moved to the keyboard next to Woody's pilot controls and hammered away in a flurry and within seconds she declared, "Done. Images are uploading to Worley now."

"Good," I said. "Can you add *Sinbad*'s cameras to our configuration here while I buzz Worley?"

"Give me two minutes," Jas said.

I dialed Worley's direct number, and he picked up immediately. "Go for Worley."

"Commander, we found the boat, and we've just uploaded some images for you."

"I'll be damned. She's really there?"

"Standing proud on the bottom like someone just parked the family car," I said.

I could hear typing on his end of the call and then he continued. "Getting the images now. It's in amazing condition," he said, "it's unbelievable. This whole thing seemed so far-fetched a few weeks ago and now . . ."

"Yeah, the reality hit us pretty hard too. We're launching *Sinbad* now."

"Good," he said. "Can you patch me into *Sinbad*'s video feed?"

I looked at Jas.

"Coming up," she said, typing away at the keyboard.

"Video feed coming up, Commander," I said.

"Excellent. We've got you on radar," Worley said. "And I've tasked a satellite that'll give us an aerial view of your position every hour."

"Good. We don't want any other visitors while we have the mini-sub in operation."

"Roger that, Captain. We'll be watching. I'll check back in a few hours," Worley said before ending the call.

Turning to Jas, I said, "I'm going to the aft deck to watch the guys launch *Sinbad*, and I'll be back as soon as they've splashed."

"I'll get the video patch to Worley up and running and check coms with Beau and Mac," she said.

Stepping out on to the work deck, Rudy and Morgan were finishing the lifting harness hookup to the submersible. A golden morning sun still hung low in the winter sky as I approached *Sinbad* sitting in her cradle and made eye contact with Mac. "You good?" I mouthed.

Mac was in pure game mode and gave me a straight faced nod and a thumbs-up. I took a step further aft on the large plexiglass dome. Beau sat in the copilot seat, heads down, engrossed in system checks. I rapped on the surface with my knuckles to get his attention. "You good?" I said.

Beau nodded, grinning ear to ear with an enthusiastic thumbs-up.

I turned to Morgan. "He's clearly ready."

"It's like you got him a new bike," he said, smiling.

"Well, go ahead, get 'em wet."

Morgan spun a finger in the air, signaling to Rudy to hoist away. In a few seconds, the lifting line became taunt and *Sinbad* lifted into the air. Rudy skillfully manipulated the lift controls, raising *Sinbad* up and over our stern rail and gently kissed the multi-million dollar submersible onto the surface of the turquoise blue water of the Gulf. The sea conditions were calm and the water clarity on the surface was gin clear. The combination of the plexiglass dome on *Sinbad*'s hull and the golden morning light made for incredible reflections and sparkles as the mini-sub settled down into the water. Rudy called to Mac on the radio, and when all systems read "go," Mac reached above his head and pulled the lever, releasing the lifting hook, allowing *Sinbad* to sink slowly under the surface.

Walking forward up the starboard side deck, I started up the steps to the pilothouse. I wanted to check on Jerry before I went back to the edit bay to observe *Sinbad*'s dive. Jerry was sitting in the helm seat, looking out the forward helm windows as the sun kept changing the colors and sparkles on the surface of the Gulf. When I stepped in, it jarred him out of his reflective trance.

"You know, buddy, it occurred to me, I haven't said thank you."

Jerry lowered his head slightly. "Michael, there's—"

"Thank you, Jerry."

"If you'd been on that roof, I have no doubt you'd done the same," Jerry said.

"Any of us would," I said. "But now, how are you?"

"It's all good, Cap."

I looked at him with a sideways glance. "How you doing, Jerry?"

He smiled and shook his head. "I'll be fine, Michael. But I ain't gonna lie. It's tougher than I imagined. I saw a lot of bad stuff riding EMT rigs in the bad parts of Baltimore, but there's no preparation for that part after you pull the trigger.

I'm thankful for all the training we've done. It just . . . took over. That man was going to kill as many of us as he could, and I couldn't let that happen."

I stood there and let Jerry's words sink in. Jerry was right, and I knew it. Although I'd fired and hit a man with nonlethal rounds; I'd never taken a life. "I understand part of what you said. On several of my assignments overseas, I saw things I've wished so many times I could unsee. Witnessing that level of loss and destruction changes a person in ways that most of the public will never know. But as bad as those things were, there was always that thin veil of separation between the ugliness and yourself. Pulling the trigger is a very different thing, yeah? Have you talked to Morgan about it?"

"I will," he said. "I'm just not ready yet. But I'm good to go, Cap. Standing at this helm is good medicine. So, I'm just going to stay busy."

I stepped up, putting my hand on his shoulder. "Understood," I said. "Thank you again. You're a good man, Jerry Styles. And a vital part of this team and this family. If you need anything, you let me know. Copy that?"

"Copy that, Michael."

There was a slight breeze blowing through the two open wing doors of the pilothouse, filling the space with the smell of ocean and a bath of morning sun. It was a gift

of a calm morning on the wide-open Gulf. I left Jerry standing at the helm in the best treatment room a mariner could
ever have.

Chapter 13

BACK IN THE EDIT BAY, Jas had the split LED screens configured with *Sinbad*'s video feed, Woody's camera, and the HIC-SA sonar array. Woody hovered at the stern of the ghostly 601 awaiting the arrival of Mac and Beau in the submersible. They were four minutes from reaching the depth of the sleeping sub. I picked up the radio and keyed the mic. "*Sinbad*, you copy?"

"We got you five by five, Captain," Beau answered.

"Mac," I called.

"Go for Mac," he answered.

"On this first dive, we're just doing recon. Copy?"

"Copy that. Recon only."

The HIC-SA display began displaying the reflections of

the approaching submersible, and twenty seconds later, Woody's forward camera gave us a view of *Sinbad*'s arrival at depth. The large acrylic dome descended into the frame, lit by Woody's lights, as it slowed to a stop fifty feet off the U-boat's large propeller . We could make out Mac perched at the forward helm controls, and he reached for the throat mic that was part of *Sinbad*'s com system.

"Surface command, mind your eyes," he called.

Jas and I looked at one another, a little confused, as the screen flashed solid white for several seconds before the auto-exposure of Woody's camera could compensate. Mac had powered up *Sinbad*'s lights, which were many times more powerful than our small ROV.

"Thanks for the warning." I laughed over the coms.

We watched as *Sinbad* slowly rotated, bringing its power-ful light array around to bathe the eighty-year-old war machine in a wash of cool blue light. The additional illumina-tion revealed an even more impressive view of the old sub through *Sinbad*'s camera.

"I still can't believe it," Jas said.

"Maybe not, but there it is," I said, before keying the mic. "Mac, let's start your pass down the starboard side."

"Roger that," Mac replied. "Easing down the starboard side."

Woody followed along behind *Sinbad*'s path, giving us a vantage of the larger submersible through its camera's lens. The new video feed coming from the submersible revealed nothing new as it scanned down the hull, but the details we could see in the steel's condition and the markings on the conning tower were much clearer. Forward of the tower, the view of the opened hatch we saw earlier was still a mystery. The additional light gave us a view into the space that made it easier to see more details. It appeared to be maybe eight feet deep by six feet wide and sealed at the bottom by a watertight hatch.

"Any clue?" I called over coms.

"I got nothing," Beau answered.

"Mac?" I asked.

"Some type of radio buoy, maybe."

"Seems too large for that," Jas said.

Sinbad continued its orbit around the sub, surveying the port side until it reached the area behind the conning tower and onto the main deck and the location of the docking collar. Mac maneuvered the submersible over the hatch, giving us an even closer view of its design and details.

"I'm going to set down on it and see if the hatches will match," Mac called.

I quickly keyed the mic. "This is just a recon dive, Mac. Let's hold off on that."

"We're here, Cap. I'm just going to set down to check for a compatible fit," he answered.

I didn't like it, but Mac was an experienced operator and

he was three hundred feet below us on site. If the roles were reversed, I'd want some operation latitude as well. "Mac, set down on the collar, but under no circumstances open *Sinbad*'s side of the air lock. Understood?"

"Understood, Captain."

My shoulders tensed as the video feed gave us a view of the submersible slowly descending down onto the 601's docking collar.

"Ten feet," Mac called. "Seven . . . five . . . three."

From Woody's camera, we saw the extended docking flange that hung under *Sinbad*'s primary hull touch down onto the U-boat's deck.

"Looks like it's a—"

Our screens went black.

The interior lights ship wide blinked twice as well, but remained on. I keyed the mic. "*Sinbad, Sinbad*, we've lost all video feeds. Do you have coms?"

Jas was madly checking systems and control connections. Not only did *Sinbad*'s feeds go black, but so had the feed from Woody's camera and all the HIC-SA data.

"Dammit," I yelled. "*Sinbad, Sinbad*. Do you copy? Beau, do you copy?" Nothing.

"I'm completely dead stick on the ROV," Jas said as she started pulling access hatches under the console to check cables and connections.

The radio squawked and an excited Jerry called out, "Cap, what's happening? We've lost everything up here, even the ship's main sonar went black."

"Not sure. Jas is troubleshooting now," I answered.

Morgan shot through the hatch into the bay. He was breathless from running from somewhere on the boat. "What's up?" he huffed. "What would have taken all our systems down like that?"

"I don't know," I answered. "How long can *Sinbad* stay under before resurfacing?"

"About eight hours," Morgan answered.

Rudy and Harper stuck their heads around the hatch to see what had caused the short light outage. The pair listened to our exchange, and Rudy peeked over one chair to see Jas scrambling around on her back under the console, digging through all the hardwired connections within our system. "Everything looks in order here. I don't know what the hell is going on. I'm going to do a hard-reset on the whole system," Jas called out.

"How long?" I asked.

"Fifteen to twenty minutes, if I can get power to the system," she answered.

"Go as quick as you can," I said.

"I'll be in my work compartment," Morgan said as he ducked out of the bay.

"I'm gettin' my shotgun," Rudy gruffed. "Come on, Harper."

My cell phone rang, and I pulled it from my pocket, glad to see we still had some form of communication. It was El-lie. She'd have to wait. I touched the screen, sending her to voicemail as I headed for the pilothouse. I hadn't made it three steps out of the editing bay before the phone rang again. It was Ellie again. I answered abruptly. "El, we're in the middle of—"

"Michael, I've got info you need, and I don't think it should wait."

I stopped abruptly on the steps between decks. "Go."

"The dark web chatter around Sleeping Wolf is there, and it's indeed a European-based neo-Nazi cell. These guys are organized and well funded. No surprises there."

I was worried and impatient, causing me to bark, "Well then, what's the surprise?"

"It's the info regarding Mac Summers."

"Kinda pressed for time here, El. What about him?

"When I started going through his background, every-thing seemed normal. Coast Guard MSRT. Grew up in the New Orleans area. Dad, Mitch Summers, was a residential contractor in the area."

"El, net me out here."

"Just listen," she snapped. "There is nothing, and I mean

nothing, on the Summers family before 1958. Not a trace. No grandfather, grandmother. No property deeds. No immigration, social security, or citizenship information."

"How can that be?" I asked.

"It's as if they popped into existence in the late fifties."

"Could his father have been adopted?" I asked, still not believing what she'd said.

"It's me you're talking to, Michael. There would be some trace and you know no matter how small the thread was, I could find it. There may be some bizarre explanation, but my gut is screaming that something is very wrong here."

I let her words sink in and I consciously slowed my breathing. I had to think. "El, that's good work. Keep digging and I'll call you back in an hour. We've got a submersible on the bottom and we've lost communication and visuals system-wide."

"Where's Summers?" she asked.

"Driving the submersible with Beau," I answered.

"Go. But call me back," she said.

"I will," I said, and ended the call.

I couldn't explain the information concerning Mac's background. The uneasiness in my gut matched Ellie's at this point. But that would have to wait. My first priority had to be getting Beau and Mac safely off the bottom. I started up the steps to the pilothouse, but stopped dead after two steps, then reversed directions in a sprint down to the guest cabin where Mac was bunked. Stepping into his cabin, I scanned the room, trying to decide where to start. I emptied his seabag onto the bed and started going through his things. Nothing seemed unusual. Next, I looked through his leather soft-side briefcase. Again, nothing suspect. A copy of his orders, couple of legal pads, some personal correspondence, and a Clive Cussler paperback. I sat on the bunk, racking my brain. This all seemed crazy. If there was something off about Mac, how did he get this far?

I looked under his bunk and pulled out a small pelican case Mac had brought aboard with him. None of us had bothered to open it. There didn't seem to be any reason to. He was an asset provided to us by Naval Intelligence. I sat the case on the bunk and flipped the latches open. When I lifted the lid, inside was a black square-shaped box with four small antennae protruding from the top. There were also two rows of LED lights. One row was red and one white. They were blinking on and off in an alternating pattern. I lifted the box from the case and turned it over, trying to find the power source. A small door with a latch was on the bottom side, and opening it, revealed a palm-sized lithium battery. I removed it, pulling loose the power leads. The lights stopped flashing. I wasn't sure what it was, but I was sure nothing in Mac's cabin should be powered up and blinking during dive operations.

I dropped the box back in the case and looked around the cabin, and decided to give the leather briefcase a closer look. I ran my fingers across all the stitched seams on the bag. Halfway down a seam on the back side, I felt a bump. Pulling out my knife, I cut the stitches on the seam and pulled it apart. Inside was a small tube about three inches long, about the diameter of a pencil. A short antenna protruded from one end and two wires connected to a small battery extended from the opposite end. *Dammit, that's a tracker.*

The evidence that Mac was something more than we knew was piling up. Now I was really worried about Beau. If Mac was involved with the extremists we'd already encountered, he was a very dangerous man. And Beau was trapped in a submersible with him in three hundred feet of water. I pulled out my phone and dialed Worley. He answered on the first ring.

"Michael, we lost the video feed, is everything all right there?"

"We lost everything ship wide here, Commander."

"What happened?" he asked.

"We're working on it. But let me back up a second. I just got a call from my sister, Ellie, and she's discovered some missing information regarding Mac Summers."

For the first time, Worley had added some heat to his already gruff voice. "Missing information? Like what?" he asked.

"Seems like the Summers family didn't exist until the mid-fifties," I answered.

"Captain, there could be a million explanations for that. Summers was well vetted for this operation," he said.

"Then can you explain why I just found some type of electronic jammer and a tracker hidden in his cabin?"

Worley was silent.

Finally, I said, "Commander?"

"And currently, you're not in communication with him, your crewman, or *Sinbad*?"

"We are blind at this time. Our tech is rebooting our systems now," I answered.

"Let me get into it," he said resigned to the bad news. "Let me know the second you reestablish contact."

"Will do, Commander," I said, before ending the call.

I grabbed the pelican along with the tracker and headed to Morgan's shop. The hatch to Morgan's room of trouble stood open, and he was inside putting together two specialized dive regulators. I dropped the case and tracker on the stainless steel worktable. Morgan stopped working and glanced at the items I'd dropped. "That's a tracker," he said. "Where'd you find it?"

"In the seam of Mac's briefcase," I answered. "Do you

know what this is?" I opened the pelican case and spun it to give him a better look.

"No, but my guess would be a black-out jammer. Where was that?"

"Under his bunk."

Morgan dropped his head and looked at the floor. "Shit."

Chapter 14

"ELLIE CALLED AND SAID she'd found some missing pieces in Mac's family background, so on a hunch, I searched his cabin," I said. "Then I called Worley."

"What'd he say?" Morgan asked.

"A little defensive at first."

Morgan scoffed, "I bet."

"He said, he'd get into it," I said.

"Someone's gettin' chewed on right now," Morgan said. "We've got to get down there."

"What's the plan?" I asked.

"Ever dive with Trimix gas?"

"Yes, once," I answered.

"This is similar," Morgan said. "We'll combine the specialized gas mixture with these rebreather systems. It'll only give us about twenty minutes at depth and we'll still need to make some decompression stops on the way up. I don't love it, but the fact that we're working blind means we're out of options."

"Let's go," I said.

My radio chirped and Jas called out, "Michael, coms are back up, but there's no response from *Sinbad*."

"How about video and ROV systems?" I asked.

"They've just accepted the reboot command and they're responding. I can have all systems back in less than twenty," she said.

"Let's get going," I said to Morgan.

Minutes later, Morgan and I stood on the aft dive platform rigged with wet suits and rebreather systems complete with full-faced masks and coms.

"A nice slow descent," Morgan said through the communication system.

"I'm following you," I answered back.

"Jas, Jerry. You have us on coms?" Morgan called.

"Coms are all back, we have you both," Jas called.

"Five by five at the helm," Jerry called.

"Video feeds are almost up. We'll have full visuals back before you reach depth," Jas said.

"Roger that," Morgan called. "You ready?" he asked me.

"Right behind you."

Morgan stepped off the platform and splashed down into the crystal blue water. He resurfaced, giving me the okay sign, and I stepped off after him. The initial splash caused me to wince as the gear straps impacted my torso, but the semi-weightlessness of the water felt good against my ribs. We confirmed we were both good to go, and we started for the bottom. Despite our anxiousness to get to reach depth, we agreed on a cautious descent rate, making it a ten-minute trip. At two hundred thirty feet, Jas's voice filled the small speakers in my mask system. "We have full visuals and ROV control. Woody drifted off station, so I'm making my way back to the 601."

"What about *Sinbad*'s camera?" I called back.

"From the camera's view, it looks like they're still sitting on the docking collar, but we can't raise them on the radio."

"Keep trying. We'll be at depth in a couple of minutes," I called.

Minutes later, we reached the bottom. Our powerful dive lights stabbed narrow shafts of light out into the darkness and soon we picked up the furrowed trail in the seafloor ten yards from the propellers of the 601. Once we reached the aft end of the grounded sub, we went up and over the prop and started forward, along the main deck, toward the docking collar. Morgan's light flashed across the top part of *Sinbad*'s

Lexan bubble. The submersible's lights were dark, but I was glad to see it was still there. Off the U-boat's starboard side, I could see our ROV, Woody, approaching, adding more light to the scene with its light array. We approached the clear cockpit enclosure, and I shined my light inside. Beau was slumped forward, unconscious against his set of aft controls. A quick spike of panic caused my chest to tighten. The forward pilot seat of the submersible was empty.

My mask's speakers clicked as Jas combined all the com channels together, allowing me to hear her attempts to raise anyone aboard *Sinbad*.

"*Sinbad, Sinbad*, do you copy? Beau, Mac, come in," she called.

I watched Beau closely for any sign of consciousness, but he didn't stir. The bright lights and reflection off the glass made it hard to get a great view inside the cockpit, but I didn't see any sign of blood or injury. Continuing to watch for any signs of life, I could see Beau's back rise and fall subtly, so it seemed he was breathing, at least. Morgan switched off his dive light and flipped it over tapping the clear bubble with the back of the pistol grip. Still, there was no movement from Beau.

"Are you seeing this, Jas?" I called over the coms.

"Yes. Where in the hell is Mac?"

"Looks like the hatch to the sub is sealed, but *Sinbad*'s

docking hatch is still open," Morgan said. "And what went there?" he continued, pointing to a space on the floor of the submersible's cockpit.

I shined my light down for a better look at the open floor hatch where Morgan pointed. "In the original *Sea Eye*, that was a battery compartment. Looks like one cell is missing," I said.

Morgan tapped on the glass of the cockpit again. This time, a little harder. We watched Beau closely. He stirred slightly this time, and Morgan doubled his efforts tapping the glass.

"Beau! Beau! Do you read us?" I called over the coms.

He rolled his head side to side. He was beginning to come around. Without raising his head completely, his weak, shaky voice called back, "Cap? What's happening?"

"You're okay, buddy. You're still in the *Sinbad*."

Beau raised his head and looked through the clear Lexan at Morgan and I with squinting, sleepy eyes. "Hey . . . what y'all doin' out there?"

"We lost contact with you. We thought maybe you guys found a pub down here and didn't invite us," Morgan said through the coms.

"What?" Beau said, still shaking off his confusion.

"Never mind," I said. "Do you remember what happened?"

Beau rubbed his face with the palms of his hands and shook his head a few times.

"I remember we were about to touch down on the docking ring. Then nothing." He looked up suddenly as it all began to sink in. "Hey, where's Mac?"

"We're assuming he went aboard the sub," Morgan said.

"He must have spiked my water," Beau said, holding up a bottle with only a few sips left in the bottom. "He handed it back to me and told me to stay hydrated, as soon as we buttoned the hatch."

"He also used something to knock out our video feeds, coms, and computer systems on *Water Horse*," I told him.

Suddenly there was a vibration on the eighty-year-old sub's main deck. I looked at Morgan wide-eyed. "Is that the main engine?" I asked.

Bubbles and silt gurgled up from the bottom and curled around the hull of the sub, rising toward the surface as the sleeping hulk of steel struggled to wake up from its decades of sleep and loosen the grip of the mud and silt.

"Whoa!" Jas called. "I'm seeing some weird action on Woody's feed. What's going on down there?"

"We think the engine on the 601 just started," I answered.

"We've got to get *Sinbad* sealed and undocked," Morgan said as he relit his light and started inspecting the seal around the docking ring.

"Beau, you've got to get that inner hatch sealed and get off this deck."

"Roger that!" he replied, as he scrambled over the back of the pilot's seat to reach the docking hatch. Beau carefully closed the hatch and spun the air lock handle, making *Sinbad* watertight.

"Can you undock and get to the surface alone?" I asked.

"I will now!" Beau answered.

The vibration increased on the sub's main deck, and the bubbles multiplied.

"Whoever's driving this thing is purging ballast," Morgan called. "We gotta move, Beau."

Jerry called over coms. "Michael, Morgan. Worley just radioed and said we have two targets heading our way. He said they look like shrimp boats on the satellite pic. They're running about eighteen knots and two miles apart, so they're not run-of-the-mill shrimpers."

"Well, this just keeps getting better," I said.

On a brighter note, *Sinbad* had managed to power up with only one of its battery cells and thirty seconds later Beau called to us. "I'm ready to release the mag lock on the docking collar, Captain."

"Roger that. We're going to have to make two decomp stops on the way up. Can you stay with us?"

"Can do," Beau answered. He pulled a lever to the right

of the pilot seat, and after a loud clank, the submersible re-leased from the hull of the 601 and floated six inches off the deck, continuing to rise slowly.

The vibration and noise of the German boat became louder, joined by the groans and creaks of aging steel. Within seconds, violent swirls of mud and silt clouded the water, making it nearly impossible to see.

"We can't be this close if this thing gets free of the mud," Morgan called. "We'll get sucked into the props."

"Hang on to the side rails," Beau called, as we both reached out for a handhold on the metal rail along *Sinbad*'s hull, only seconds before our visibility decreased to zero.

Even through my face mask, I could hear the submersible's electric motors whir to life, and it pulled us away from the 601, off its starboard side. The deep pop, pop, pop of steel changing shape after years of stillness was now accompanied by the deep whumping of a large prop, its blades biting for purchase against the water. The sounds vibrated against our heads and chests, but it was impossible to see what was happening. I estimated that *Sinbad* had pulled us maybe thirty yards from the sub, before the spinning electric thrust motors went quiet.

"Beau, I can only see your lights," Jas called. "I'm moving Woody along with you off your starboard side." It was good to hear a voice from the surface in our now completely snow-blind condition in the murky water.

"Copy that," Beau answered.

"Let's sit tight for a minute and see if the visibility will improve before we head topside," Morgan said.

The noise and vibration from the antique U-boat gradually decreased, and slowly the water clarity improved. Reflexively, Morgan and I pointed our dive lights in the direction we last saw the X-601, along with the lights from Woody and *Sinbad*. As the silt, sand and mud settled to the bottom, we all stared in utter disbelief at what we didn't see. In the spot where an intentionally grounded WWII submarine rested for eighty years, there was nothing more than a giant depression on the seafloor. The advanced U-boat was gone, with no other trace than the wispy trail of mud disappearing into the blackness along its northerly headed wake. No one spoke as we floated there, dumbfounded.

"That's a hell-of-a-thing," Beau said, snapping us out of our daze of disbelief.

Chapter 15

"Let's head topside," Morgan called. "Our first stop is at two hundred feet."

We kept a one-handed grip on *Sinbad* as we rose toward the surface. I called Jerry over coms. "Jerry, do you have the approaching target on our radar yet?"

"I do, Cap. They're eighteen miles out."

"Roger that. We're on our way topside, but have to make two stops. Keep us updated."

"Get weapons," Morgan called.

"Already there," Jerry answered. "Rudy and Harper have been on patrol since you two splashed."

We all chuckled.

"We need to get up there," I said.

Our two decompression stops seemed like an eternity, taking us fifty minutes to get within ten feet of the surface. Jerry called back, "Boys, we've got one of the approaching boats in sight, maybe you shouldn't maneuver up to the platform just yet."

"We're not leaving you there!" I shouted back over coms.

"Looks like a crew of eight and they're armed to the teeth," Jerry replied.

"Dammit," I said through gritted teeth.

Sinbad's bubble broke the surface forty yards off the stern of *Water Horse*, and Morgan and I broke the surface seconds later. We could see the shrimp boat approaching from the southwest, but we floated so low in the water, so I hoped the crew on the shrimp boat hadn't detected us. There were only three crew members aboard *Water Horse* and those were bad odds against eight heavily armed radicals. By the time we reached the boarding platform, they'd be close enough to fire and board us, just as we'd be climbing aboard and rushing to get to our weapons.

Beau's voice came through our coms. "Morgan and Michael, swim over and hold on to Woody. Jas, can you maneuver Woody and pull away from *Sinbad* with the guys holding on?"

"Yeah, but why?" she called.

"I have a really bad idea," Beau said.

"This can't be good," I muttered. "Hey, Beau?"

"I got this, Cap," he answered, over the sounds of a series of switches being flipped.

Morgan and I pushed off the side of *Sinbad* and swam the twelve feet to where Woody floated on the surface. We each grabbed a buoyancy tube on either side of the ROV and Morgan called to Jas, "We're on. Go, Jas."

Woody's motors whirred up with a high pitch whine, and the small machine towed us aft, out and away from the semi-surfaced submersible.

"We're forty yards off, Beau. What's on your mind?" Morgan asked.

"FIRE IN THE HOLE," Beau called before *Sinbad* torqued hard to port followed by the whoosh of one of its mini-torpedoes shooting out of the launcher from craft's starboard side. It streaked just under the surface toward the shrimp boat still steaming toward *Water Horse*. Morgan and I looked at each other in complete amazement, then looked back at the silvery trail barreling straight for the shrimp boat.

"Incoming!" Morgan yelled through his headset. "Water Horse, take cover!"

Two seconds later, BOOM! An explosion erupted at the waterline on the aft end of the attacking vessel's starboard side. The blast instantly crippled the boat, and with its engine silenced, the damaged hulk drifted to a stop. The impact would certainly sink her, but it may take hours. Armed crew-man scrambled forward on the side decks, trying to escape the fire and smoke near the area of the torpedo strike. Seconds later, a second explosion erupted up and out of the boat's aft working deck with a raging tower of fire and smoke, sending debris hundreds of feet in every direction. Morgan and I quickly submerged several feet, taking shelter from the burning bits and pieces of the wooden boat that rained down across the surface of the water. When the debris settled, we both surfaced to see what little remained of the shrimp boat sinking rapidly under the surface, with flames burning what was left of the hull and cabin.

"What in the hell do you think was in the hold?" I asked.

"Something allergic to fire," Morgan answered.

The flames hissed and popped as the water quenched the burning wreckage, section by section.

"Water Horse, everyone okay there?" I called on the radio.

From where I floated on the surface, I could see Rudy on the port side deck of *Water Horse* dowsing bits of flaming debris with a fire extinguisher. Rudy called over his radio. "We're all good here, Cap. We'll have some paint touch-up to do."

"Cap, we still got another bogie heading this way," Jerry called. "They'll be on us in less than twenty minutes."

"Roger that, Jerry. We're on our way," I answered.

"Hang on," Jas called, as ROV's motors spun up again and towed us toward *Water Horse*'s swim platform.

"Beau, you have enough juice left to maneuver to the boat?" I called.

"On my way, Cap," he answered, as *Sinbad*'s forward bubble pushed a small wave of water out in front of its course toward our aft swim deck.

Woody coasted to a stop within arms-reach of the boarding ladder and I scrambled aboard. Morgan stayed in the water to help with the recovery of the submersible. Rudy was already at the crane controls, spooling down the cable as Jerry led the harness end toward the rail, ready to hand off to Morgan. Harper stood with his front feet on the port rail, somehow sensing the direction the second boat would be approaching. His low growl was audible all the way across the work deck. I called over my coms before pulling off my face mask. "Jas, call Worley and give him a sit-rep. We've got to go after the 601 as soon as we get everyone aboard."

"Roger that."

I peeled off my face mask and regulator rig, and left them with my fins in a heap on the work deck.

Rushing back to the dive platform, I helped pull the rebreather rig off Morgan's back and onto the platform.

Gathering his gear, I climbed back up on the deck and piled his gear with mine.

"You got this?" I yelled down to Morgan as he reached to receive the lifting clamp that was lowering down to him in the water. *Sinbad* was only seconds from arriving.

"I got this. Go get some weapons!" he called, as the submersible got within reach and he began climbing up onto *Sinbad*'s top to connect the lifting rig.

Still in my wetsuit, I ran toward my cabin and stepped into the already open door to find Jas tossing my tactical vest onto the end of the bed. Her vest and side arm were already on her. Without speaking, I raised my vest up to slip it over my head. Pain exploded up my left side like a violent electrical shock. "Awwh!" I gasped. The combination of the adrenaline and floating in the water almost made me forget about my injury.

Jas stepped up and pulled the vest into place over the wetsuit, then secured the side straps. She handed me a SIG semi-automatic butt first. I took it, ejected and checked the magazine, before sliding it back into place, then slid the handgun into the holster on the front of my vest. Jas handed me a com set with earpiece and throat mic, and I put it in place in my right ear.

"I brought the HK416 from the pilothouse, plus two extra mags."

"Perfect," I said as she handed me the Heckler & Koch.

"You good?" she asked, putting her hand on my chest.

"I'm good. No one comes aboard this boat."

"You got that right," she said, as she pulled the sling strap of her matching assault rifle over her head.

It was after three in the afternoon when Jas and I stepped back out on the aft deck. Rudy, on the crane controls, was just setting *Sinbad* down onto its cradle, with Morgan perched on top. He spun the handle to the upper hatch, then lifted it, allowing Beau's large frame to crawl out of the submersible. Jerry had vests and weapons organized on the bench against the aft cabin bulkhead on deck.

"I put kits for both of you over there," Jerry said, pointing, as he tightened the last strap securing one of *Sinbad*'s skids to the cradle.

Morgan and Beau trotted to the bench and donned vests and weapons.

"We've got two survivors in the water," Jas called out, looking over the port rail out into the debris field of the shrimp boat.

Two men with black oil-stained faces and burns on their exposed forearms clung together on a collection of fishing buoys from the deck. Morgan threw a life ring with a line attached in the men's direction. One of the men managed to hook his burned arm through the loop of the ring, and Morgan pulled the line, reeling the pair aft toward the dive platform.

"Get the med kit," I called to Jerry.

Morgan, along with Jas, shouldering her weapon, watched the men closely as they climbed the boarding ladder up onto the swim platform.

Morgan spoke in a calm, even tone. "Nice and slow, men."

The two men climbed the short ladder up onto the work deck under Jas's close cover.

"You have them?" Morgan asked her.

"Oh yeah," Jas said.

Morgan went over to one of the lockers on the aft deck and returned with four sets of large zip ties and instructed the men to have a seat. The two men stared stoically straight ahead as Morgan zipped tied each of the men's hands in front and zipped tied one leg each to opposite ends of the bench that was securely bolted to the deck.

"Jerry, against my personal desire, will you give these two silly Nazis a shot to take the edge off these burns. They have to be pretty painful."

Jerry was reading Morgan's mind. He was already drawing a syringe with a clear opiate of some variety. Jerry injected the first man into his upper arm without a single reaction. He drew another syringe of the painkiller from the vial and went to the second man. He injected the second man in his right arm and withdrew the needle. The man broke his stare and looked at Jerry, more resigned than his partner.

"Thank you," the man said in perfect English.

"Four miles out at eight o'clock," Rudy shouted, pointing to a spot on the horizon.

We all looked in that direction, and Harper echoed Rudy's alert with a few deep barks and growls.

I keyed my com mic. "Water Horse. The red light is on. Everyone move into position to repel boarders."

Everyone dispersed to their assigned positions as the approaching boat steamed on a direct course for our position.

I was back in the pilothouse, and Jerry was back in his nest on the cabin roof, when I called out. "Jerry, you have eyes on?"

"I do, Cap. Not a shrimper this time. Looks like an oil rig crew boat. I count seventeen . . . no, eighteen crewmen, all armed but the pilot. Two miles out."

Eighteen men. That was too many. My brain madly searched for an idea that might give us any advantage. And seconds later, an advantage showed up.

Morgan joined me in the pilothouse before stepping out onto the port side wing deck. He'd retrieved the shoulder-mounted rocket launcher he'd borrowed from the enemy's cache on the shrimp boat.

"Told ya it might come in handy," he said.

I picked up the mic to the VHF radio. "Crew boat on a northeast heading, approaching blue-hulled expedition ship. Do not approach any closer or we will assume you are hostile. I repeat, gray-hulled crew boat, do not approach our vessel or we will assume your intentions are hostile."

There was no reply. Now at just under two miles out, with binoculars, I could see the crew boat's bow pushing a winged silver wake of water, occasionally sending spray up and over their bow rail.

"Just under two miles out," I called to Morgan out on the wing deck.

"I got 'em," Morgan said, peering through the sights of the shoulder launcher.

When the crew boat reached one mile from our position, I called to the crew. "Water Horse, the crew boat is one mile out. Everyone—"

"INCOMING!" Morgan yelled into his coms, cutting my transmission short.

I dropped to the deck, pain shuddering through my upper body as I slammed against the floor and covered my head with my arms. I didn't know if we were the target, but Morgan's alert sent everyone diving for cover.

There was a short high-pitched whistle followed by an enormous explosion and shockwave that rattled the pilothouse windows. I was afraid of what I might see when I painfully pulled myself up from the deck. Still crouching, I peered through a pilothouse port for a look. The explosion reduced the crew boat to nothing more than smoldering flotsam on the water's surface. There would be no survivors this time.

Chapter 16

MORGAN STEPPED BACK INSIDE the pilothouse. "Ha, I still have this!" he said, cradling the rocket launcher. "I may get to use it yet."

My cell phone rang from the chart table, and I crossed the pilothouse to answer it. It was Commander Worley.

"A little unexpected, but I like your timing," I said, after accepting the call.

"Took some doing, but we got approval for a Predator drone run. Your crew all okay?" he asked.

"We're all good, Commander."

"I saw the video feed from your ROV. I don't know what to say yet. Summers passed all the background checks, plus all the vetting he had to do for his MSRT work. But mostly I'm a little embarrassed that I judged him to be a good man," he said.

"We all did, Commander. But we'll worry about that later. We need to find that sub. We'll be underway in two minutes," I said.

"Hold on," Worley said, as the commander obviously placed his hand over the phone to muffle the conversation happening at the ops center.

"Captain, we tasked the drone to run constant surveillance over the area between your position and the river entrance," he said. "We have the submarine on the surface, and a pilot boat met it nineteen miles from your position. Looks like he took at least three people aboard. They're back underway, making eight knots."

"Looks like they're running the Sleeping Wolf Protocol by the book," I said.

"We've also got two small fast-attack boats standing by," Worley said.

"It'd be great to stop the boat before you had to destroy it. But I know it has to be stopped at all costs," I said.

"Yeah, we'd all like a look inside that boat, but we can't let it get close to the city. I'm going to have the Coast Guard stop river traffic for a routine safety check for the next eight hours," Worley said.

"Roger that. Send us any position updates you have." I ended the call.

I picked up the mic to the ship-wide intercom. "Water Horse, secure for flank speed."

I took the boat out of hover mode and slowly pushed the throttles forward and the deep thrum of our main engine began pushing us northward toward the entrance to the Mississippi River. In a little over a minute, we were cutting through aqua blue water under the late afternoon skies at fourteen knots.

We were about ninety miles from the outer buoy, and at this speed, it would take us six and a half hours. I didn't know how Mac managed to get the sub off the bottom alone, but I knew he probably knew these local waters as well as any man. A flurry of other questions ran through my mind. If he knew he'd been discovered, would he try to launch the V-2 rockets on New Orleans instead of going further inland? Did he take on any other weapons from the pilot boat along with the extra manpower?

I turned to Morgan. "Worley said they have the sub on surveillance from the drone, and they it met up with a pilot boat and took on more crew."

"But still, how in the hell did he get the sub off the bottom by himself?" Morgan asked over my shoulder.

"I can't wait to ask him that, from a cuffed sitting position," I said.

Morgan raised his hand, pointing through the front pilothouse window. "And how are they making eight knots in a floating time capsule, for crying out loud?"

"What I'm trying to figure out is if Summers is what you would call a 'true believer,'" I said.

Morgan stood thinking about that one for a few seconds before shaking his head thoughtfully. "I've dealt with a lot of them. All over the world. And I gotta say, he had me fooled."

"I think he had us all fooled," I said. "Ellie to the rescue . . . again."

"We'll never hear the end of it." Morgan laughed.

Beau stepped into the pilothouse, looking surprisingly alert. "You look ready to go," I said."

"I got a hell-u-va nap down there," he said, smiling.

"You really good?" I asked.

"Oh yeah, I'm ready to catch us a slippery Cajun. One a Jerry's kin would say, 'Goin' choot da feesh.'" He laughed.

"Jerry's gonna choot your feesh, Marine."

We all laughed.

"Well, if you're really good to go, stand a helm watch. I'd like to get out of this wetsuit and wash the salt off," I said.

"Me too," Morgan echoed.

"Go, I got this," Beau said.

"It'll take hours to catch up to them, as long as they don't increase their speed," I added.

"I'll ring as soon as I see anything on radar," Beau said.

In my cabin, I threw my coms set on the desk and somehow managed to escape from the tactical vest. But the wetsuit zipper was a challenge. I reached behind my back through the stiffness to grab the strap attached to the zipper pull like I'd done a million times. But intense pain shot through my left side when I twisted. After several tries, I dropped my arms to my sides in defeat. *I'll just cut this damn thing off.* I looked over at the desk for my pocketknife when I felt the zipper catch slowly pull down my back. And the tightness of the suit release.

"Never thought I'd need to unzip your dress," Jas said in a hoarse whisper over my shoulder.

"May have saved my life," I said. "You, for sure, saved this wetsuit. I was seconds away from cutting it off."

"Well, I hope this was better," she said.

I turned to face her. She was still wearing her vest and side arm. I leaned forward and stopped with only a breath between our lips. I waited two long seconds, then gently kissed her. "It was better. Thank you," I said. "If I'd called Morgan, I'd never hear the end of it."

"You would not," she agreed. "Go get cleaned up. Rudy's making sub sandwiches. Come to the galley when you're done. No telling when you'll be able to eat again."

"Roger that," I said, turning for the shower and peeling out of the wetsuit. A catcall whistle rang out over my shoulder just before the click of my cabin door being pulled shut.

It was just after dark as I sat in the galley, eating like a man who hadn't had a meal in days.

"Need me to put that sam-ich in a respirator for you?" Rudy asked. "You're supposed to use your teeth."

"It's good and I'm hungry, you old salt. Back off, or you may draw back a nub."

Rudy laughed. "I saved you some of my banana puddin' in the fridge," he said, ducking out of the galley hatch, headed for his shop. "If the jackals haven't found it," he finished, his voice trailing off.

My phone rang, and I pulled it out of the front pocket of my vest that I had put back on over a clean T-shirt. It was Ellie.

"What's happening? You were supposed to call," she asked seconds after I hit accept.

"It's been a full couple of hours, Sis."

"Was I right?" she asked.

"Beginning to look that way," I said. "Mac drugged Beau and boarded the U-boat. Then somehow managed to get it off the bottom, and is currently heading toward New Orleans."

"He's what? The sub's operational? How's Beau? Are you going after him?"

"Yes, that really happened and apparently the boat still runs. Beau is fine, and we're in pursuit now and hope to catch up to the sub soon," I said, recapping her litany of questions.

"Then what?" she asked.

"Stop the sub before it reaches New Orleans," I said with great confidence.

Her next question instantly transported me back home as a fifteen-year-old, trying to get out of showing our folks a bad report card.

"Michael, how are you going to stop a sub?" she asked, sounding like the twelve-year-old that was already smarter than Morgan and I both.

"The plan is a little fluid right now, but we're working on it," I said.

"Oh, good, a fluid plan," she said. "I just texted you a picture."

My phone pinged, and I touched the alert. A photo of a boy and what seemed to be his father and grandfather filled my screen. The boy, maybe ten years old, proudly wore his baseball jersey with "Crawdads" in script across his chest, above the number eleven. The boy's father looked in his early thirties, and the man I guessed might be his grandad looked in his eighties. I blew the photo up on my screen cen- tered the picture on the oldest man's face. I froze.

"That's impossible," I whispered.

I flipped through my phone's photo app until I found the

pictures I'd taken in the hold of the shrimp boat. There in the black-and-white photo of the U-boat captain was the square jaw and the eyes I remembered. But the look clinched it. Pure, uncompromising determination. I'd seen someone recently with that identical look.

"What's impossible?" she asked, snapping me back to the present.

"Who is this?" I asked.

"I kept digging through old newspapers and school announcements in the area and I found this photo from the town paper at the kick-off to little league season one year. The photo didn't identify the older men, but it identified the boy as Mac Summers, pitcher for the Crawdads."

After a pause, I said, "I think grandad in that picture is Hans Schreiber, captain of the X-601."

"How is that possible? He would have died eighty years ago," Ellie said.

"Unless he didn't."

Chapter 17

JERRY STUCK HIS HEAD AROUND the galley hatch frame. "Cap?" he whispered. "Beau needs you in the pilothouse."

"El, I gotta run," I said.

"Wait . . . Michael—"

I ended the call.

I followed Jerry up to the pilothouse. "What's up?" I asked.

"We've got a target heading straight for us, dead ahead," Beau said, pointing to the radar screen.

Checking the target's reflection on the radar, along with the range scale, it showed something approaching five miles out and closing fast. "It's not the sub," I said.

"No, looks like a regular boat signature," Beau replied.

"I'm about fed up with boats making a run at us," I said, before keying the mic on a radio. "Morgan, you have ears?"

"I'm up and running," he replied.

"You still want to use your borrowed shoulder mount?"

"Happy to oblige," he said.

"Rudy, will you and Jas relocate our guests on the aft deck to inside one of the aft cabins and secure them?" I called.

"With pleasure," Rudy said.

"Rudy, remind Harper we're just moving them. Copy?"

"He'll be disappointed but understood, Captain," he answered.

Fully dark now, the three-quarter moon made the approaching boat easy to see on the horizon, even though it was approaching, without running lights. Looking through the binoculars, I could see it was a pilot boat approaching. It had to be the boat that off-loaded crew to the sub. I picked up the mic to the ship-wide radio. "Water Horse, hostile approaching, take cover. I don't think there's any question of their intentions, but everyone just keep your heads down for now. We'll let them make a pass first," I called over the radio.

Another glance through the binoculars didn't improve the outlook. Our approaching boat of hostiles was still closing fast. We'd be bow to bow with them within three minutes.

"What do you see?" Beau asked.

"Can't tell how many men are on board. But the boat looks just shy of fifty feet," I said.

Still watching, the boat closed to within two hundred yards, then altered course enough to pass down our port side. "Six men," I said. "Assault rifles, pointing out their port side windows."

When the boat closed to fifty yards, and without slowing, they opened fire.

"Incoming!" I called over the radio. Our crossing speed would be almost forty knots, so they wouldn't have long to hit anything. The gray-hulled pilot boat passed down our port side twenty yards away, in a barrage of gunfire. Rounds pinged and ricocheted off *Water Horse*'s steel hull, before falling silent as it passed beyond us.

"Everyone okay?" I called.

"All good, Cap," Rudy called. "Are we gonna shoot back next time?"

"You bet ya," I answered.

"They're circling around for another pass," Beau called. "Coming up our starboard side this time."

"They'll be passing slower this time," I called to the crew. "Be ready."

I peeked around the frame of the starboard pilothouse door to watch their approach, as the pilot boat gained on us.

But even with their much greater speed, the smaller boat bounced and wallowed as it clawed its way over our large stern wake. The darkened windows of the pilot boat revealed nothing about who or what might be inside as they continued shortening the distance between us. They would likely open fire any second. When they'd closed to within fifty yards of our stern, Morgan strode straight out across *Water Horse*'s aft deck and up to the stern rail on the starboard side. Automatic weapon fire erupted from the pilot boat.

"Return fire!" I called as our team returned the favor, firing back at the approaching boat. I stood mouth agape as Morgan calmy raised the shoulder-mounted launcher, oblivious to the rounds whizzing by him. He steadied the launcher, aimed, and a flash of fire preceded the smoking streak of the rocket as it tore from the barrel toward the pilot boat. The trip took less than three seconds before the projectile struck the front of the pilot boat's enclosed helm station, followed by an enormous explosion. All weapon fire stopped and the charging boat's forward motion slowed to a stop as it veered off course to starboard, completely engulfed in flames. Morgan lowered the launcher and walked calmly back toward the aft cabin entrance.

"Now that's what I'm talking about," Rudy called over the radio.

"Should we circle back around?" Beau asked.

"No time," I answered. "I'll call it in to Worley, but we need to catch a sub."

I dialed Worley, and he picked up immediately.

"Go for Worley."

"Commander, we just left a pilot boat that tried to intercept our pursuit in flames. We have no status on survivors," I said.

"I'll get a boat on the way. We're monitoring your position."

"Do you still have eyes on our U-boat?" I asked.

"We do. Still running on the surface, just under fifteen miles in front of you, and they've increased their speed to ten knots."

It was going to be close. At their current speed, we'd catch up just as the sub was approaching the outer entrance markers of the river. "Commander, if you haven't already, launch the fast-attack boats," I said.

"Already done. They're just over three hours away from the entrance buoys," Worley replied. "The boats have the fire-power to keep the sub from coming deeper into the channel, if that's what it takes. But we really don't want a sea battle in the mouth of the Mississippi River."

"Understood. If we can get close enough, we can force him aground," I said.

"Good luck, Captain. We'll be monitoring your progress and be watching your back."

"Thanks, Commander," I said and ended the call.

"Force them aground?" Beau asked with a raised eye-brow. "You just make that up on the spot?"

"Fake it till you make it," I said.

Beau shrugged his shoulders nonchalantly and looked back out the forward windows, continuing to man the helm. "Describes most of my life," he replied.

Feeling the pressure, I pointed to the throttle level. "Give us a little bump there."

Beau looked at the main engine tachometer and back at me. "Rudy'll fuss."

"He'll be fine. He'll monitor the engine temps and grant us a little grace. He knows what's at stake in this chase," I said.

"Roger that," Beau said and nudged the throttle forward a touch, trying to squeak out another knot of boat speed.

Morgan stepped into the pilothouse along with Jerry, Jas, and Rudy in tow. The whole crew was here, anxious for what was next. "Nice shot," I said to Morgan.

Morgan shook his head sadly. "They wouldn't have stopped."

"I know, Brother."

"How we gonna stop that sub?" he asked.

Beau looked back at me with a smirk, waiting for my answer.

I cleared my throat and turned up the confidence. "If we can catch the sub before he's too far in the channel, we can come alongside and force him into shallow water, and run him aground. The boat likely has five or six feet more draft than *Water Horse*. As soon as they get close to the channel, they'll have a navigator in the conning tower in contact with a helmsman. A little cover fire will keep him distracted."

Morgan nodded thoughtfully. "Not bad."

"Pretty big game of chicken," Rudy said.

I open my hands, palms up. "I'm open."

"I've got one rocket left. If we can get close enough, I can try to take out his prop. If I miss, we just risk blowing up the whole sub," Morgan said.

"Between those two, I'd love to hear a plan C, but I've got nothing," Jas said.

Forcing the sub aground, would work, but it would put *Water Horse* at serious risk of damage, if not holing and sinking us. I trusted Morgan's skill with the rocket launcher, but one rocket was one shot. No room for a miss. I considered both options before looking up at the group and saying, "We'll call taking out the prop with the remaining rocket, plan A and the big game of chicken, plan B."

Nods of agreement came from the group.

"As soon as we're in range, I can launch a drone and give us some eyes on things, well before we catch them," Jas said.

"Depending on how recent they've done any dredging in the entrance, there'll be shoals near the channel. We can spot some good places to beach him from the air before we arrive," Jerry said.

"That's good," I said. "Great planning. Jas, get the drone ready, with Beau assisting with the launch. Jerry, I want you at the helm for our approach. Rudy, we'll launch the RIB the second we get the sub stopped, one way or another. Then Morgan and I will take the RIB and board the sub."

"With Beau," our marine said.

I looked at Morgan, and he nodded. "With Beau," I finished.

Chapter 18

WE WERE T-MINUS THREE HOURS from catching up to the old German U-boat. We'd detect them on radar in half that. The crew was busy preparing gear for the A-B plan we'd all agreed was our best shot at success. Now, it was just the dreaded waiting before our plan kicked into action. Most captains were all too familiar with the old adage of "no battle plan ever survives first contact with the enemy." But I wondered how many captains had dark moments of doubt in the quiet before the storm. I knew I did. Despite my desire to run assignments that didn't put our crew and boat in danger, here we were.

Even knowing that teams of horses couldn't keep my team away from what we were trying to do, I felt the weight of responsibility for each of them and their safety. But we couldn't allow someone to fire rockets into New Orleans or get as far as Baton Rouge and fire rockets further inland. It would send the nation into panic. Immediately following 9/11, the nation came together. But now, over two decades later, the nation felt more divided and polarized. An attack in our heartland would likely bring the exact reactions all terrorist desire, panic and fear. The fast-attack boats could likely destroy the sub in the mouth of the river, but even they're no match for a V-2 rocket, antique or not. Just the news of an armed battle with terrorists that close to a population center could trigger a wave of national fear. We had to stop it before that happened.

With Jerry already at the helm, I made my way down to the camera shop. I paused in the doorway and watched Jas fine-tune one of our long-range drones. Her ponytail hung loose through the hole in the back of her Water Horse ball cap. I was fond of the look.

"You about got that ready to go?" I asked, stepping up beside her.

"Be ready to fly in ten minutes," she said. "How about you? Are you ready to storm a German U-boat?"

"I am."

"Maybe we should let Worley and his team finish this one. You're still hurt, Michael," she said turning to face me.

"Nothing more tape and three Advil won't fix," I said.

She shook her head. "We still have that date for a talk, remember?"

"Oh, I do. And I'll be there," I said, reaching for her hand, but she pushed against my chest.

"Go on, get out of here. I need to finish this. Morgan's down in his locker putting your gear together. As soon as Jerry picks the 601 up on radar, I'll launch the drone and send the video feeds to the helm."

"I like the hat," I said, reaching to touch the side of her face.

"Why do you think I wear it?" She smiled. "Now get outta here," she said, turning back to her work on the drone.

Morgan stood inside his locker we affectionally called the "tomb of trouble," preparing a few additions to our kits we'd use to board the 601 if we could get her stopped.

"Nothing exotic this time, Brother," Morgan said, without looking up. "Just bullets and flash-bangs this trip."

"I think Summers is the grandson of Hans Schreiber, captain of the X-601."

Morgan's head snapped up. "What?"

"Ellie kept digging and found an old little league photo from an archived newspaper. The pic showed Mac as a kid with his father and a man that I'd bet a thousand bucks was a much older Hans Schreiber," I said. "You saw the look on his face in the photo we found in the hold of that shrimp boat. Would you forget that look?"

Nodding, Morgan answered, "Pretty memorable. But how?"

"I don't know," I answered, shaking my head. "That opened hatch that was forward of the conning tower has been bothering me."

"An escape pod, maybe?"

"Seems unbelievable, but all this seems unbelievable," I said.

"Mac said his grandfather was ninety-three when he died, so it's possible, I guess," Morgan said. "But Schreiber's dead now and his 'maybe grandson' is not, so we'll start there."

"Agreed. What do you have for us?"

Morgan placed two stacks of mags on the worktable. "Extra mags for your SIG and the HK and four flash-bangs each."

"Night vision?" I asked.

He slid a set of night vision goggles across the table to me.

"Now all we have to do is convince a German U-boat to pull over." Morgan grinned.

I snapped my fingers in the air. "Piece of cake."

Jerry called out over the radio. "Cap, I've got 'em on radar. Ten miles out."

"Roger that. Keep me updated. I'll be in the edit bay until we're closer." I keyed the radio mic, "Jas, are you and Beau ready to launch the drone?"

"Beau is on the work deck now. We're ready," she answered.

"Launch it and let's get some eyes on this situation," I called.

"Eyes on the way," she said.

Morgan and I geared up and headed to the edit bay, just in time to see the drone lift off the aft deck, revealing a shot of *Water Horse*'s deck and running lights getting smaller and smaller in the camera's frame as the drone gained altitude. Morgan and I each took a seat in the leather easy chairs, watching the show unfold on the large monitors. I watched as the on-screen telemetry from the drone showed it'd reached an altitude of three hundred feet. Then the drone's camera tilted up and the remote vehicle sped ahead at fifty knots in search of our fleeing submarine. The moon was near full, And although the video feed was dark, you could clearly make out the horizon and the moonlight sparkling off the water far below.

"It won't take long to reach them at this speed," Jas said over her shoulder as she sat at the console piloting the drone.

We all sat glued to the monitors as the drone shortened the distance to the target every second. Three minutes later,

Jas pointed to the monitor. "There," she said. "Top of the screen, see the stern wake?"

"Got it," I said.

"I'm flipping to night vision," she said, and the monitor flashed a few times transitioning the images into monochrome shades of green.

"When did you add that?" Morgan asked.

"We added lots of things while you were away," she said, smiling over her shoulder.

Morgan looked at me, and I shrugged my shoulders and nodded my agreement.

At this altitude, combined with the sound of the surface-running sub, the drone would be undetectable to anyone in the conning tower. The drone closed on the U-boat's position and the camera tilted downward as it flew directly above the fleeing boat.

"Looks like you were right, Brother. There's someone in the conning tower," Morgan said, watching the footage closely.

Nodding, I said, "Water will be getting skinnier soon, and I'm sure Mac's local knowledge of the area's depths and shoals are valuable."

"They're still running ten knots," Jas said.

"Let's hope they don't speed up when they realize we're behind them," I said.

"We'll know soon enough," Morgan said. "How much time till we're on them?"

"Just over two hours," I answered.

We watched for another few minutes, but the vantage didn't change. The X-601 and its conning tower lookout were running a steady ten knots on a course straight for the outer entrance buoys to the river.

"Let's go get the RIB prepped for launch," Morgan said.

"In thirty minutes, I'll need to come back for a battery swap," Jas said. "But I can get here and back on station quick."

"Understood," I said. "We're on coms."

Out on the work deck, Rudy had already removed the cradle straps that secured the inflatable, *Pinto*, and had the lifting harness in place. The menacing gray-and-flat-black painted boat looked like an armored medieval warhorse under the working deck's bright lights. Its twin two-hundred-fifty-horse outboards tipped forward, anticipating their chance to churn up some salt water. Morgan stepped up onto the side of the cradle and over into the cockpit. I handed him our matching HK assault rifles one by one and he secured them. Next I handed up a backpack with a med kit and various survival gear. I lifted a second bag up to Morgan, and he asked, "What's in this one?"

"Camera gear, of course," I said.

"Optimism, I like it," he said, stowing the gear.

We checked and rechecked the boat's systems until we were sure *Pinto* was ready.

Above us, we heard the buzzing of our drone's six props, sounding like a swarm of angry killer bees, as it descended for our aft deck.

"Incoming drone," Beau called.

When the craft got close enough, Beau assumed flight control from his better sight line out on deck. Using the remote flight controls, he guided the drone down and landed it with a gentle kiss on the deck. The props spun down, and he sprinted over to the airframe with a fresh battery. He made the change in seconds and trotted back to the controller, and the drone lifted quickly back into the night sky, where Jas would resume control and head back to the U-boat's position. She'd be able to provide great aerial surveillance as we attempted to overtake the sub.

Just before midnight, Morgan and I headed for the bridge to watch our pursuit approach. Once inside the pilothouse, Jerry pointed to the radar. "They'll be making the turn at the outer entrance marker to the southwest pass pretty soon, Cap."

I looked at the range of the target on the radar and compared it with the nav chart. The sub was just over the horizon from our sight. When the sub made the turn into the channel, they'd be off our radar, as the entrance jetty would block the reflection. Even when we got them in sight, we'd lose them until we could make the turn into the channel ourselves.

Jas called over the radio, "The drone's back on station, Captain."

We all turned our attention to the video feed on the helm console as the drone resumed its position three hundred feet above the U-boat, with its camera pointed straight down. The lookout remained in the U-boat's conning tower. After several more minutes observing the sub, we all held our breath as the sub made a wide turn slowly to port to line up for the entrance to the channel.

"There's the outer marker," Jerry said, pointing through the front window of the pilothouse. Seconds later, the sub disappeared from radar as the U-boat passed behind the jetty.

"We're catching up," I said. "Rudy," I called on the radio.

Rudy answered back in a loud voice, trying to overcome the noise of the main engine in the background. "Go for Rudy."

"Can you give us a few more hundred RPM? We almost have them in sight," I said.

"Push it to the stops, Captain. We look good down here. Just try not to run her there long."

"Roger that," I called, then gave Jerry a nod, signaling him to push the throttle to its stop. The vibrations under my feet increased as *Water Horse*'s powerplant wound up to its maximum output. Our speed slowly increased to just north of fifteen knots. The additional strain on the main engine wouldn't make a huge difference in our speed, but every second that we might gain felt like precious currency in added options and opportunities to stop something terrible from happening.

"Captain, check the monitor," Jas called with clear excitement in her voice.

The three of us looked at the monitor, showing the drone cameras, but couldn't believe what we were seeing. The X-601 was veering off to starboard, heading for a shoal that extended from the earthen jetty wall.

"You seeing this?" Jas called.

"Yeah," I answered. "Just not believing it."

We all watched slack-jawed, as the U-boat continued to veer out of the depth of the main channel, and finally, its forward motion slowed to a stop as it grounded on the mud and sand of the shoal.

"What are they doing?" Morgan said.

"Beats me, but I'm not gonna look a gift horse in the mouth. Getting that sub stopped was the hardest part of this whole fandango," I said.

The group's eyes stayed glued to the monitor as the drone held position over the grounded U-boat.

"Jas, take the drone lower for a closer look," I called.

"Coming down," she answered, as the view from the camera descended, drawing closer to the boat and leveled off at one hundred fifty feet. From this vantage, we could see the conning tower was now unoccupied and the hatch leading below was open.

We were minutes from reaching the river entrance buoy and making our turn to port. Then we'd have the U-boat in sight. What made them stop? Did the sub have mechanical problems? They could reach New Orleans with their V-2 rockets from here. And it would be easier than navigating the river. If that was their play, the devastation would be horrific. I knew we had to get there first, and the clock was ticking down in a heart-racing blur.

Chapter 19

I watched both the drone camera feed and our distance to the entrance marker. When we reached the green-lighted buoy, Jerry began our slow turn to port, bringing us into the channel. There, two miles ahead of us, I could see the silhouette of the submarine's conning tower on the far east side of the channel under the moonlight. We kept our deck and running lights on, and I watched the drone monitor carefully to see if there was any movement around the conning tower hatch as we'd be visible now to anyone watching. We were just over a mile away now, and I put my hand on Jerry's shoulder.

"As much as I want to get there, I don't want to spook them into taking any rash action. Bring us down to idle speed."

Jerry eased the throttles back and said, "Rudy will love you for that."

"Rudy," I called on the radio. "Beau, and I are heading aft. We're ready to launch *Pinto*."

"I'll be at the lift controls in thirty seconds," Rudy answered.

Beau and I left the pilothouse and on the way down the starboard wing deck steps, I called over my shoulder, "This is a little too easy, right?"

"We're not there yet, Brother," Morgan answered as we made our way aft along the main deck.

"Yeah, I know," I said. "I just never thought the sub would stop on its own. We don't usually catch that kinda break."

Morgan stopped and turned to me. "It's been my experience that in most battles, about the time you think you caught a break, one foot is standing in a cobra hole."

"Noted," I said, as we continued aft.

Reaching the work deck, Beau was there waiting for us, geared up and ready.

"Jas says she can recover the drone herself, so we're good to go," Beau said.

With all our earlier preparations, we just had to board the RIB and wait for Rudy to splash us over the side. I called the pilothouse over my coms. "Jerry, if you'll bring us to a hover, Rudy will splash us."

"Roger that, Cap. Slowing to a hover," he answered, as *Water Horse* slowed.

While we stood in the cockpit, Rudy lifted us up and over the rail, and positioned the RIB six feet off the water while Jerry brought the boat to a full stop. Rudy would splash us the instant we were ready.

"We're in hover mode," Jerry called.

"Put us in, Rudy," I said. And *Pinto* lowered down into the calm water.

Beau turned the key, starting the twin engines, and they responded instantly with a throaty purr. We let the motors come up to temperature while Morgan and I released the lift rigging.

"Hey, Cap?" Jerry called. "We've got four targets headed down river coming this way at a high rate of speed. They're five miles out."

I looked at Morgan. "Don't say it."

"Didn't say a word." He smiled.

"Jas, you have enough battery to come off station there on the sub and tell us what's coming our way?"

"Can do," she answered. "Moving upriver now."

I tapped Beau on the shoulder. "Let's go."

Beau leaned into the throttles and the big twins growled, digging into the water before shooting the RIB forward on a direct course toward the grounded sub. The water in the river entrance was calm, and we'd cross the short distance to the U-boat in under ten minutes. Halfway into our crossing, Jas called over our coms. "Okay, boys. Commander Worley's attack boats are in pursuit of two para-military looking RIBs carrying four men each. They'll be on your location in eight minutes."

Two minutes later, Beau pulled back the throttles to idle. Morgan and I shouldered our assault rifles in anticipation of anyone on board detecting our arrival as we coasted up to the port side of the sub, halfway between the conning tower and the stern. I couldn't believe the condition of the near century-old U-boat. Marine growth and rust were present, but the X-601 was remarkably preserved. As we provided cover, Beau tossed a line with a grappling hook up onto the deck and it held fast against a section of deck railing. He tied the line to our starboard side rail, then retrieved his HK from the aft locker.

"I guess there's only one thing left to do," Beau said, giving a head motion toward the rope.

"You two up first," Morgan said. "I'll cover."

I handed my weapon to Beau and slipped on the backpack with the camera gear before starting up the rope. After I made it to the deck, I lay on my stomach and Beau handed me our weapons. I stood and shouldered one rifle, covering the entrance to the conning tower as Beau helped Morgan aboard. With weapons pointed, the three of us proceeded forward on the deck toward the ladder leading up the side of the conning tower.

When we reached the base of the steel rungs, I slipped the sling of my primary over my head and started quietly up the ladder. Morgan and Beau stood back several feet, trying to provide cover fire. They couldn't see into the tower, but a few short bursts from their HKs would encourage a quick retreat for anyone peeking over the edge. In the distance, I could hear gunfire. Worley's team must have engaged with the boats they were pursuing. If the chase was still on, they'd be here any minute. When I reached the top of the ladder, I knew that when I first stuck my head over the top, I'd be vulnerable to anyone waiting inside the tower. I pulled my SIG from my thigh holster, took a deep breath, then, leading with my shooting hand, raised up enough to see into the tower.

It was empty, and I exhaled deeply, relieved a radical nut job hadn't been waiting for me to stick my head up. The hatch on the floor of the tower leading down into the interior of the sub was standing open and light poured up thru the steel hatch. I turned and gave Morgan and Beau the okay sign, and Morgan and Beau started up the ladder. With the three of us in the conning tower, Morgan whispered over his throat mic coms, "Can you hear any movement below?"

"Not a peep," I said.

Morgan knelt and lowered his ear to the open hatch. He looked up at Beau and me and shook his head. "I don't hear anything, but we can't chance it. I'm going to drop a flash-bang and I'll climb down as fast as I can behind it. Follow me down."

We both shook our heads in agreement. Morgan pulled a flash-bang from his vest and pulled the pin, paused a two-count, before dropping it down the open hatch. We turned away and held our ears as the concussion grenade thundered inside the sub, sending smoke and a bright white shaft of light through the hatch. Before the reverberation subsided, Morgan vanished down the hatch, leaving Beau and I scrambling to stay close behind. When I reached the bottom of the ladder, Morgan was already providing cover. As the smoke cleared, I saw a man lying on the deck a few feet from the base of the ladder. I looked at Morgan and pointed to the man. He shook his head, no.

I knelt for a closer look at the man; someone had killed him with a single shot to the forehead. The sub's working lights were on throughout the interior and as we took in our surroundings, it looked like a scene from a Halloween spook house. Although the interior lights were on, many were out and sporadic pools of light spilled across macabre scenes throughout the sections of the sub. The members of the original crew were still here on duty, many of them still sitting at their station. Others sat leaned against bulkheads, knees drawn up in a fetal position, still wearing their uniforms. Their dried, shrunken heads hung down, chins resting on bony chests. One man cradled a journal in his lap, a pen clasped loosely in his skeletal fingers. On the open page, a shaky scrawl in German recorded the man's final thoughts or message to a loved one. We made our way to the bridge of the U-boat, finding more bodies of the original crew, but we also found two more men of our generation. Bullets had struck both men in the chest; they lay there on the deck in pools of blood among their near century-old fellow sailors.

"What the hell happened here?" I whispered.

"Any sign of Summers?" Morgan asked.

Beau shook his head, before he whispered, "Nothing."

I knew from my research that the captain's quarters were just forward of the con on the port side. I pointed in that direction with my SIG and stepped into the small passageway. Ten feet down the narrow corridor, a hatch door stood open on the left. On the deck, a foot stuck partially out of the opening. Whoever it belonged to wasn't moving.

Handgun raised, I crept quietly toward the open hatch. Morgan's hand touched my shoulder, signaling me he was on my six. Although diminished by the subs hull, the sounds of rapid staccato pops of automatic weapon fire broke the silence of the warships interior. And the increasing volume signaled only one thing, the battle raging outside between the fast-attack boats and the men on the RIBs was getting very close. Three feet from the hatch, I froze. My brain went to work on the sound and, as unlikely as it seemed, it had to be pages turning in a book. Morgan tapped me twice on the shoulder and I took the last two quiet steps before I'd have to clear the unseen cabin. Reaching the edge of the hatch frame, I took a deep breath, then swung my body, leading with my gun arm, into the entrance of the room, ready to fire.

My eyes took in the closet-sized cabin, the open compartment door on the bulkhead, a small painting leaned against the wall poised to tip off the tiny desktop. The prone man and owner of the protruding feet lay on the floor with a gunshot wound to the chest. And there was Mac Summers sitting in a wooden chair at the desk mounted against the bulkhead. His eyes stared fixed to an open journal that sat next to a forty-five semi-automatic with the hammer cocked.

Chapter 20

MAC TURNED TO FACE ME, but made no sudden move for his weapon or to defend himself as he stared down the barrel of my 9mm.

"I just couldn't do it," he mumbled.

Morgan stepped in the doorway behind me and between the feet of the man lying on the floor with a gunshot wound to the chest. He leveled his weapon at Mac's head.

"Mac, I'm going to reach over for your side arm there on the desk and then we'll talk about it. Okay?" I said.

Mac looked at me again. He seemed dazed but still made no defensive moves. Keeping my SIG raised, I reached over to the desk and picked up the handgun and handed it to Morgan.

Lowering my gun, I asked, "Mac, can you fill us in here a little?"

Mac sat staring down at the journal for a long time, before he raised his face to look me in the eye. "My grandfather was everything to me. I loved my dad. He's a good man, but he never understood me. And he never . . . really believed in anything. It was Poppy that taught me about honor and commitment. He loved being a submariner and he never forgave himself for punching out in the escape pod. But he was more driven by the Allied bomb that killed his first wife and daughter."

"Is that what the sprung hatch was?" I asked.

"Yeah. Most of the crew had already died before he decided to use the pod. Starving, he drifted offshore for three more days before he was close enough to land to swim after sinking the escape capsule. His English was good. His father studied in the States after the First World War and insisted that his son learn to speak 'the universal language' as he called it. It served him well. He got work in the shrimp boat fleet in the area. And bit by bit, he built a life and became Henry Summers."

"But Mac, why . . ."

"Betray my country and try to finish his mission?"

"Yeah, that," I said.

"The last three or four years he was alive, he had trouble

sleeping. He never talked about his past. My dad said his mom passed away two years after he was born, and my grandfather raised him alone. Dad would always say Poppy was a private man and never talked about his past when he was a kid. Poppy told my father that his parents died when he was young and just left it at that. One spring afternoon, we were shrimping together, and he just started opening up about the past. By the end of the day, he'd told me the whole story. The way he described the motherland. The strength, power, and pride of the German people. As a thirteen-year-old boy, I was fascinated. He told me about his first wife, Sophie, and his daughter, Anna. He loved them very much and their death left him with a deep bitterness. I found an old letter from Anna he kept here in the safe," Mac said, pointing to the opened hidden compartment. Then one summer, he sent me to a summer camp in Germany that my dad thought was just an exchange student program, but it was actually a training camp for the movement. Poppy found the group online and reached out to them by including some old Sleeping Wolf code words in his message and someone in the organization picked up on it. When they discovered who he was, the Sleeping Wolf Protocol was reborn. That was fourteen years ago."

"This has been in the planning this whole time?"

Mac nodded. "I went back to the camp two times during

high school and joined the Coast Guard right after graduation."

I stood listening, still not believing how Mac's incredible story wound up with us standing here in the captain's quarters of an eighty-year-old German U-boat that somehow was still operational.

"That last couple of years I spent with him, I became obsessed with bringing him some kind of peace. When I looked at the apathy and lack of honor and commitment I saw in our country, it made me want to be part of something bigger. Something like what Poppy described in his youth in Germany. I told him I wanted to complete the Sleeping Wolf mission, and just like that, we began. I knew the Coast Guard would give me access to information and procedures I'd need, so I enlisted. But later, after I advanced to an MSRT team, things started changing for me. I could see cracks in the rhetoric of the movement. The more I witnessed the motivations and actions of the men around me during my time there, the cracks became canyons and the views of the radicals came into focus in a whole new way that terrified me. It wasn't about national pride, it was just about hate."

"You found honor and commitment in the Coast Guard?" I asked.

Mac looked back down at his lap. "I did," he answered.

"The men and women I worked with were amazing. They were all examples of everything I wanted to be."

"But you kept going?" I said.

"I was in too deep by then. These are scary people. I knew they'd kill my mom and dad if I backed away. They wiped out whole families if someone was suspected of having doubts during the planning period."

"I'm assuming this is your work," I said, pointing down at the man lying on the floor.

Mac nodded. "I had to stop it." Then he looked up suddenly. "Is Beau okay?"

"Yeah, he's just out there, in the con."

Mac looked relieved, then shook his head. "I don't know why it took so long, but I started realizing all the things that I admired about Poppy and his feelings for his country . . . I found myself feeling that about my country. I'd like to believe that at his core my grandfather was a good man. He loved me and my father. But grief is a powerful poison. And even the most noble and heartfelt beliefs can be absolutely wrong."

"Better late than never," I said. "Do you have enough intel to stop all this?"

He looked up to face me. "I know it all. I can burn it all to the ground."

"That's what it's going to take," I said.

"Michael, I know I'm headed to prison, if not worse. And even that can never make up for what I've done. But this is a cancer that runs deeper than you can imagine. We've got to stop them."

I looked down at the floor, nodding.

"FREEZE!"

The command caught us by surprise, and Morgan jerked his head around to identify the source of the voice, then raised his hands in the air, realizing there was no way for him to turn and fire before he'd be shot at close range.

Mac yelled, "*Kamerad, ich habe die Situation unter Kontrolle. Ich bin in den Kapitänsquartieren.*"

Mac gave me a wink. "Hand over the gun and raise your hands," he said.

I paused and locked eyes with Mac. If there was ever a time that I wanted to believe my gut was right, this was it. I flipped my SIG around, extending the grip to Mac. He took it, and pointed it at my chest. I raised my hands.

"Ahh, Brother, what the . . ." Morgan whispered out the side of his mouth as the armed radical approached him.

"Drop your weapon on the deck and kick it over here," the voice said to Morgan. Morgan paused, then carefully bent down and dropped his SIG on the deck, kicking it toward the sound of the voice.

I stood stone still and listened as the footsteps of the man approached. I couldn't see, but I could hear him push Morgan further down the corridor before stepping behind me. A deep voice came from over my left shoulder, "*Kamerad Schreiber, endlich treffen wir uns.*" (Finally we meet.)

Mac smiled back for a moment, and every muscle in my body tensed like steel. I stood so close to Mac's outstretched hand, I could see his right finger whiten as he took up the slack on the trigger. My ears began to ring as every second slowed to a crawl. Mac's eyes shifted ever so slightly to my left before jerking his aim over and firing. I spun around in time to see the man drop his arms, still wearing a puzzled look on his face below the bullet hole in his forehead. His body crumpled onto the deck.

I turned back to face Mac as he lowered the weapon, flipping the handgun back around, presenting me with the grip. I finally released my breath. I took the SIG and placed it in my holster.

Mac sat back down in the chair with a blank expression. Morgan darted back toward the con and yelled, "Beau?"

I followed, and we found Beau in a heap at the base of the ladder. As we reached him, he sat up groggily rubbing the back of his head. Morgan knelt next to him. "You good?"

"These bastards seem intent on me getting more beauty sleep. Are they trying to tell me something?"

We all chuckled. "You really okay?" I asked.

"I'm fine. Just an egg knot on the noggin," he said, getting back to his feet.

Mac walked up beside me, and Beau pulled his side arm with amazing speed, aiming dead center of Mac's chest.

I held my hands up. "Whoa, Beau, it's all good."

"The hell you say," he said, not yielding his aim.

Morgan put his hand on Beau's shoulder. "Stand down, Marine. He's with us, sort of."

Reluctantly, Beau lowered his SIG, but not his intense game face directed in Mac's direction.

"For what it's worth, I am sorry, Beau, and I'm glad you're okay," Mac said.

"It's not worth much, but maybe I won't shoot you, yet."

Mac smiled. "Fair enough."

Jerry called out on our coms, "Hey boys, you good over there? You missed a helluva gun fight out here."

"What's your status?" Morgan answered.

"We're all good. For once, we just watched. Worley's boys mopped up out here. One boat tied up to *Pinto*, and one man made it up the conning tower before the fast-attack crew could get him. We got worried when he disappeared inside the tower."

"He's no longer a threat," Morgan called.

"Roger that."

"We'll be back aboard shortly," I said. "I'm assuming Worley is on his way."

"He's a half hour out," Jerry answered.

I unslung the camera bag and went to work capturing images of the sub's interior. Further aft in the crew area of the boat, more expired sailors lay curled in their berths. The state of the bodies made it impossible to tell if the end came in the form of a capsule of poison or if they opted to just fall asleep when starvation ran its inevitable course. The Navy would have engineers and photographers combing every inch of this boat within the hour, but there was no way I would pass on this opportunity to capture this slice of unknown history. I shot as many images as I could before Jerry called out, "We've got Worley's boat approaching."

"Roger that," I answered, as I began stowing my camera gear.

"That's our cue fellas," Morgan said, motioning toward the hatch ladder.

Beau went up first, and I followed, with Mac behind me and Morgan bringing up the rear. When we all had descended the ladder down the sail to the main deck, Morgan pulled a set of flex-cuffs out of his vest and turned to Mac. "I'm not your judge or jury, but we need to do this," he said, raising the cuffs.

"Understood," Mac said, raising his hands together so Morgan could put the flex-cuffs around his wrists.

Morgan put his hand under one of Mac's cuffed arms and helped him to sit, leaning against the conning tower. Beau and I stood watching Worley's boat come alongside the sub as the eastern sky was showing the first signs of dawn. After securing the launch to the sub, two crew members positioned a boarding ladder against the U-boat's hull, and Worley made his way aboard. The old navy commander approached, shaking his head as he took in the sight of the U-boat that shouldn't exist.

"Good job, Captain. Pretty big fish to land," Worley said.

"Wish we could take the credit," I gave a head nod back to Mac sitting cuffed on the deck. "But he stopped the sub."

Wide-eyed, Worley asked, "He just stopped?"

"Yep, and neutralized the terrorist crew he took aboard."

Worley looked over my shoulder at Mac. "He say why he's wrapped up in all this?"

"Long story, but for what it's worth, he probably saved our lives, and he's prepared to help you take down the entire network."

The commander looked down at the deck, shaking his head. "It's a damn big mess," he said.

"Yeah, but we're standing on a big piece of it," I said.

"What's it like below?"

"Just as unbelievable as the rest of the story," I answered.

Worley smiled and nodded. "I can't wait. You and your

team will need to be debriefed. Head upriver and tie up at the terminal. Shouldn't take more than a few days and you guys can get some shore time and good food. I'll make a few vehicles available to you."

"Sounds good, Commander," I said as I extended my hand and we shook. "She's all yours."

I walked back and stood in front of Mac. "Good luck to you. You did a good thing today. And thanks for having our back below."

Mac raised his head to face me. "Fair winds, Michael. You've got a good ship and a great team. Take care of them."

"I will." I nodded.

"I'm almost glad I didn't shoot you," Beau said with a smile.

"Take care, Beau. You're a damn fine sailor, for a marine."

The three of us walked aft on the main deck to where the RIB was tied. Beau and I climbed aboard while Morgan retrieved the grappling hook and line before jumping aboard. Beau started the engines and eased us away from the steel time capsule from another era. We all took another long look at the sub as we slowly pulled away.

"Think we'll ever be able to tell our grandkids about this?" Morgan asked.

"Doubtful," I answered. "It'll all depend on how they spin this."

Beau slapped the bag of camera gear on my back. "There's always all this," he said.

"Just never know." I smiled, as Beau buried the throttles, jumping *Pinto* up on plane, headed for home aboard *Water Horse.*

Back on board, the crew busied themselves stowing gear and preparing the ship to get underway for Worley's Naval Intelligence base at the terminal. I was tightening the final straps securing the RIB to her cradle when Jas's voice called over my shoulder, "What's a sailor have to do to get a proper sitrep around here?"

I stood and turned to face her. "Bad guys, neutralized. All hands accounted for," I said, sounding official.

She poked my bad ribs. "You are such a jerk." She smiled.

"Awww. Will you stop doing that?"

She took a quick glance around the deck and stepped closer, looking up at me with her emerald-green eyes. "I'm really glad you're home, Captain. Buy a girl dinner in town?"

"You're on," I said.

Chapter 21

Two days later, I stood in the backyard of a Lakeview neighborhood. Earlier in the day, Jerry called his mom and within hours, they pulled out all the stops to host the Water Horse team to a Cajun cookout for the ages. Music poured out of opened windows on the back of the house into the backyard of the middle class home where Jerry and his brothers had no doubt climbed the tree I was leaning against. There were a dozen tables covered with heaping bowls of shrimp, crawfish, potatoes, corn, and steaming pots of jambalaya. Kids played on the edges of the yard from the multitude of uncles, brothers, and cousins that laughed, hugged, and welcomed our brother Jerry back into the fold like only a southern family could. There were iced washtubs of beer always an arm's length away and lots of dancing. Rudy wouldn't let all this cooking go on without him, so he stood behind a grill, wearing a New Orleans Saints apron, flipping a rack of ribs, and telling lies to the young shrimpers that gathered around him, enamored by the stories of the old salt. Rudy was happy as a clam. Harper roamed from group to group, trying his best to look pitiful and under fed. The barbecue sauce that matted the hair around his snout was a dead giveaway of his foraging success. Over on the patio, Beau consulted with two of Jerry's cousins, hoping to pick up any new Cajun-ese, he might use to torture Jerry.

I smiled as I stood admiring what could be a painting of "the American family." It reminded me of home and the shindigs my folks held in our backyard around birthdays, or any other reason to celebrate. Ultimately, it was days and gatherings like this that made everything we did worth it. The danger of losing this way of life would always need to be defended and protected. But today, in this backyard, it was safe.

Jas stood with Jerry across the yard, her long tanned legs descending out of a pair of well-fitted cargo shorts. The pair talked with a woman that looked to be in her early sixties. Jas must have sensed my gawking and turned to catch me looking at her. She gave me the crooked little smile that started whatever this was between us. She was amazing, and the aroma of my cooked goose was hard to hide.

Morgan took a sip of his beer before asking, "You two have the talk yet?"

"What talk?" I asked, looking surprised.

Morgan gave me the look.

"Not yet, but its imminent."

"She's something else, Brother."

"She really is," I said, continuing to watch her.

Jerry walked the pair over to where we stood. "Michael, Morgan, this is my momma, Suzannah."

I extended my hand. "It is an honor to meet you, Mrs. Styles. You raised a good man."

Jerry's mom stepped forward and pulled me into a hug and when she released me she kissed me on the cheek and held my arms as she faced me. "Please call me Suzannah, Michael. My Jerry sure loves serving on your boat. Thank you for taking care of him."

I blushed. "He's family to us too, Suzannah. We're lucky to have him."

"Thank you for all this," Morgan said, motioning to the epic hospitality that swirled around us.

"It's been a while since I was able to spoil one of my boys." She smiled.

"Well, you've certainly spoiled us today," I said. "It's very appreciated."

"Come on Momma, I want to introduce you to Rudy," Jerry said, leading his mother in the direction of the grill.

"He's a celebrity." I laughed, watching the group of young men surrounding Rudy.

"A folk hero to those young captains, I imagine," Morgan said.

I took a pull off my very cold beer and Jas asked, "What do you think they'll do with Mac?"

"Not sure. It's a pretty complicated situation. But words like treason elevates things to a different level of big-boy jail," I said.

"If he can provide enough actionable intel to bring down the entire organization, he may get repurposed, instead of prosecuted," Morgan said. "Weirder things have happened."

"Repurposed?" I asked

"I've worked with operators that, in any normal world, would be in prison. But the intel, skills, or relationships they had inside certain factions made them more valuable in the field than in jail or sealed in a black site somewhere," Morgan said.

"Do you think Mac is a good man or a bad man?" Jas asked.

I thought about that one for a minute. "I think family is a powerful thing. Just look around you," I said, as we watched the bonds of this family scattered across the backyard that were as tangible as the ground we stood on. "At the end of the day, he did a good thing."

Morgan held up his beer, and the three of us clinked the necks of our bottles. "Fair winds, Mac," he said.

"Fair winds," we echoed.

The next morning at nine, the Water Horse Expeditions team sat around a large briefing table inside the Naval Intelligence center disguised as an old river terminal building. Commander Worley stood at the head of the table. We'd enjoyed some much needed downtime, but the commander had obviously not. Tracking down the remaining cell members and their ties into their European factions had only intensified since we handed over the X-601, and the lines on his face showed the added wear and tear.

A large screen showed a video link established with Ellie, as she was required to attend the debrief as well.

"Hey kids! How are all my peeps?" Ellie said over the video conference connection.

"We're good, Sis," I said. "Once again, great research work, thank you."

"Yeah, your girl got skills," Ellie said. "Jas and I keep you knuckle draggers out of the technological stone ages," she said.

"Preach!" Jas said.

"Yeah, yeah, we know. What's the daytime high temp in NYC right now?" I asked.

"You had to go straight there, didn't you?"

Worley broke up the verbal razzing, by raising his hand. "All right, good morning, Water Horse. I hope you enjoyed your day ashore. Before we get started, I need to remind you about the nondisclosures you all signed. The situation is further reaching than we originally estimated and intelligence security on this has risen to 'top secret.' Nothing that occurred in the last week surrounding this incident can ever leave this room. Is everyone clear on that?"

Nods came from around the table.

"Ms. Gannon?" Worley asked looking to the video conference camera.

Ellie looked like a kid being called down in class. "Ah, yes sir, understood."

"Naval brass and Homeland Security have made the decision to keep any information about the terror network as classified," Worley continued.

"They don't think the public should know what's going on here?" Morgan asked.

Worley shook his head. "We don't know how far-reaching the network goes. We can't chance it. When they feel like they have eliminated all of the threat, they will consider releasing a sanitized version of the incident."

"Has Mac's intel been helpful?" I asked.

"Yes and he was right, Captain. It appears he has it all. It will be the biggest takedown of a terrorist network in the last fifty years. We have involvement from Interpol, MI-6, and German foreign intelligence," Worley said.

"And the X-601," I asked.

"A month from now, the Water Horse Expeditions team will discover an exciting marine archaeological find. While on assignment for the Naval History and Heritage Command, your team discovered an old B-17 bomber named . . ."

Shocked, Morgan and I exchanged looks. "The Li'l Nell," we said together.

Worley continued, "As your team increased its search area into the debris field of the B-17 sight, your sonar hit another target which turned out to be the unmarked U-boat."

I raised an eyebrow and leaned forward like I was about to ask a question.

Looking me straight in the eye, Worley said, "Any and all details of the U-boats advanced design or capabilities will remain classified."

I sat back in my chair. "Understood, Commander."

"And due to the unusually good condition of the sub, the Water Horse team decided to also turn that find over to NHHC and naval researchers to study and properly preserve this incredible piece of history."

"We're good guys, like that," Morgan said.

The group laughed, and Worley continued. "A major New York newspaper will break the story, written by Eleanor Gannon."

"Get the hell out-a-town!" Ellie called.

I big-brothered her. "El."

"Sorry." El sat up a little straighter in her chair. "That's an incredible opportunity, Commander Worley. Thank you."

"Naval Intelligence and Homeland will approve every word of the story before publication. Any leak or unapproved details surrounding the sub will be in breach of the nondisclosure. Do you understand the ramifications of any violation, Ms. Gannon?"

For the first time since I could remember, Ellie looked a little intimidated. "Yes, Commander, I understand."

"Good. This is an ongoing operation that's going to reverberate through the intelligence community for a while. I cannot stress enough how locked down everything you've all seen and heard must remain, along with any details related to Operation Sleeping Wolf. We are working with German intelligence to repatriate the remains of the German sailors," Worley concluded.

Morgan spoke up. "Commander, our team understands perfectly what's at stake here."

Worley smiled and shook his head. "I trust you do, but I had to say the words."

I stood. "I'll have Jerry get with your admin team to wrap up our business, Commander. We'd like to shove off this afternoon if our debrief is complete," I said.

"That's just fine. I had my team top off your fuel last night. You're good to go."

"That is very generous, Commander, thank you," I said.

"Your team did excellent work, Captain."

I stood and addressed our crew. "Guys, let's get the boat ready and we'll push off for Stock Island before noon. El, thank you. I'll call you when we get underway."

"Get my cabin ready. I'm heading down when you get back," she said before signing off.

The team stood and started toward the exit. Jerry stepped up looking a little nervous.

"Cap, I think I'd like to take your offer and stay in New Orleans for a week or so. Would that be okay?"

I put my hand on his shoulder. "If you don't, I'll fire you. It'll be an easy trip back to the Keys, and we have plenty of hands. Stay and get caught up with your family and we'll see you when we see you."

"Thanks, Michael. I didn't realize how much I missed 'em."

"Call me when you're ready and we'll book you a flight," I said.

We shook hands and Jerry headed outside.

"Michael, Morgan, can you two hang around a few more minutes?" Worley asked.

We both sat back down and Worley walked to our end of the table and sat against its edge.

"I've been asked to gauge your interest in working with Naval Intelligence on future assignments," the commander said.

"Sir, it's not our desire to fight terrorists for a career. Water Horse Expeditions is a research ship for hire. My brother and I left our previous jobs to avoid this level of conflict on a regular basis," I said.

Worley smiled. "Call me Ed, Michael. I understand your position. Yet it seems you find your way back into that breach on a regular basis."

"Guilty there, Brother," Morgan said.

I shook my head. "I don't know, Ed. We're not a military unit and don't want to be."

"Door kickers we have. What we need is smart, versatile teams that can operate covertly in the open and have the skills your team members possess. You keep taking every research project you can find. We'd just like the opportunity to reach out to you when your capabilities match the job."

"I'd want the ability to say yes or no to any assignment and to walk away from anything I think is too risky for our team," I said.

"Understood," Worley said. "And as a gesture of thanks and trust, I've also been authorized to perma-loan you the *Sinbad* as a part of your research arsenal."

Morgan and I exchanged looks. "I'm glad Beau isn't here. He'd say yes and offer to wash your car for life," Morgan said.

We all chuckled, and as it subsided, I extended my hand to our new friend, Commander Ed Worley. "Ed, when the job is right, and we're needed, please call on Water Horse. We'll be there."

Chapter 22

AT SIX THAT EVENING, I sat at my desk. Golden sunlight, reflecting off the Gulf, poured through the bulkhead port, flooding my cabin in a warm glow. My laptop stood open as I scrolled through the pictures I'd taken aboard the 601. We'd encrypt the files and store them on our secure back up system, then wipe any trace of the files from every other device.

As I scrolled, I kept stopping on the images with the remains of the German sailors, each of them frozen in time. I thought about the men's last days and moments aboard. They were the enemy, and eighty years ago, they intended harm to our country. But the curled forms leaning against bulkheads and lying in berths revealed a fragile humanness. When you peeled away the twisted ideology, they were just men. Reflecting on my career's war zones assignments, it sure seemed like the first thing forgotten by the men, women, and groups trying to kill each other was the fact that we're all just people trying to get to that family cookout in the backyard. I didn't have any illusions that geopolitics could be more complicated than that, but I couldn't help but wonder how many times we made conflict a complicated trigonometry problem, when simple addition and subtraction might bring the peace.

We'd been underway and southbound for a little under six hours. I looked forward to getting back to Stock Island. I was already craving a hogfish sandwich, and hoped that I could make an agreement with Randy Tyson to moor *Water Horse* on a section of his seawall. It'd be nice to establish a safe base for the team and give us all a place to heal and get stronger for what may come next.

Reaching in the cabinet below the desk, I pulled out the bottle containing the last two pours of Powers and two rocks glasses. The bottom of the bottle held just enough for two small shots, and I carefully drained it into the glasses. It was a beautiful evening with temps in the low seventies. The seas were calm, and it was shaping up to be a beautiful sunset. I had a hunch where Jas would be, and taking the two glasses, I headed to the bow.

She stood leaning against the starboard rail, watching the sinking sun turn from yellow to red as the watery horizon tightened its grip on the day. I walked up beside her, leaning on the rail and putting my shoulder against her. I could feel the warmth of her arm against mine and again that sensation of soothing warm oil began spreading through my limbs and chest. My brain offered a few alarms when it realized I was becoming hooked on the feeling. But alarms or not, I knew I wanted to feel more of it. I handed her a glass and we both took a sip, silently watching the western sky.

"That's the last two pours, until we get home," I said.

"Home?" she asked.

"Yeah, I'm just trying on that word for a bit. How's it sound?"

"Well, for me, *Water Horse* is home. But I can't think of a better place to tie it."

We both drained our glasses, letting it warm our insides, complimenting the setting sun's warmth on our cheeks. It was a perfect evening and it was time, so after a deep breath, I said, "Jas?"

"Michael, I need to tell you something," she interrupted.

"Shoot," I said.

"I got an email yesterday from Vertical Blue."

"What's that?" I asked.

"They govern the world free-diving championships at

Dean's Blue Hole in the Bahamas." She paused a beat before continuing. "They've invited me back to compete and attempt to break the current free immersion dive record. I came so close in my last competition, before I left the sport."

"And you left because of the relationship with your coach, right?"

"Mostly," she said. "But I was also just ready for more."

"Do you want to go back?" I asked, turning to her.

"I feel like I left some unfinished business there."

"The same coach?" I asked, trying to make my question sound like fact finding rather than any concern about what would happen if she hoped to pick up where they left off.

She put her hand on my cheek. "New coach to help me get back in shape. Then just me, to see if I have what it takes to finish what I started."

"Sounds better already," I said. "How long would you be gone?"

"Two or three months," she said, looking down at her feet.

"When would you leave?"

"As soon as we're back. I'm going to have to play catch up for the first few weeks," she said.

"Three months is not so bad," I said. "Beau is miles from your capabilities, but he can probably muddle his way through."

Jas looked up at me. "Is that what you're worried about?"

"No," I said. "I'm just trying to act cool. Is it working?" I drew my left arm up and protected my left side. "And please don't poke my ribs again."

Jas smiled. "I'll cut you some slack. But you're wrong you know."

"Several times a day, I'm sure. What's it this time?"

"These weren't the last two pours of Powers on the boat. There may be another in my cabin. Why don't I grab it and stop by your place in a bit? We still have a scheduled talk, yeah?"

"Well, I wouldn't mind one more short drink," I said, watching the horizon as the sun tucked itself under the horizon, slipping away for the night.

Jas stepped close and kissed me on the ear, whispering, "I'll be by shortly." Then she left me on the bow with my thoughts.

I just stood there grinning like a schoolboy as the last sliver of the sun slipped beneath the fiery-bathed waters of the Gulf.

Late the next day, I tossed a line to a gray-bearded Randy Tyson, standing on his seawall outside of his woodworking shop on Stock Island. He made the line fast on one of the large bollards on the wharf left over from when his place was a commercial fishing landing. Beau and Morgan helped secure the rest of the lines, and Rudy dropped our boarding steps into place. I crossed over to the seawall, and Randy and I shook hands. "Randy, I appreciate you working with us. I think we're gonna be right at home here," I said.

"To tell you the truth, feels good to have someone tied up here."

A woman, wearing a pottery apron covered in clay smudges and streaks, stepped out of the workshop and approached us. "You must be Captain Gannon," she said. "I'm Yvonne."

"Very nice to meet you, Yvonne," I said.

"I made you something," she said, as she handed me a beautiful cobalt-blue coffee mug with the Water Horse Expeditions logo embossed on the side.

"It's beautiful," I said, admiring the color and depth of the textured glaze she'd used on the mug. "My guys are going to be jealous."

"Oh, I'm throwing some for them too. They'll be ready in a few days."

"It's what she does," Randy said, proudly.

"Well, thank you so much and we really appreciate the hospitality. If there is anything our team can do to be helpful, just name it," I said.

Yvonne turned and headed back into the shop. "Shrimp boils on the first Friday of the month," she said over her shoulder.

"Don't want to miss that," Randy said as we shook hands again.

"This bunch of boat rats? We'll be there for sure. Thanks again, Randy."

"Welcome home *Water Horse*." Randy smiled, before turning back for his shop.

I crossed back over to our main deck and climbed the steps to the pilothouse. Morgan sat in the helm seat, reading some of the technical material on our new submersible, the *Sinbad*.

"Hey there," he said. "We all squared with the Tysons?"

"All good. Very nice people. Look what she made for me," I said, raising my new mug.

"Nice!" he said.

"Studying up on the new gear?" I asked.

"With Jas out, I think we'll need more than Beau up to speed on the ins and outs of that beast. It's an amazing machine."

"Good thinking," I said.

Jas stuck her head inside the port pilothouse hatch and looked over at me. "Give a girl a lift to the airport?" she asked.

It hit me harder than I thought. It was real now. She was leaving. "I'll call us a taxi and ride with you. Will you give me twenty minutes?"

She looked at her watch. "That'll work. Meet you on the dock," she said and ducked back out of the hatch.

I stood there quiet for a few seconds before Morgan spoke. "You have the talk?"

"We did," I said.

After not offering any further details, he punched me in the arm. "Well?"

"We'll see what happens in three months," I said.

"And your good with that, after your very successful Marilyn Wilson prom strategy? " he asked.

"Ouch, that's low, Brother," I said. But the jab struck a nerve that surprised me as I bolted up into a taller stance. "You know what? I'm not," and I tore through the pilothouse hatch and made for my cabin.

Twenty minutes later, I walked out on the main deck toward the boarding steps. Morgan met me before I climbed the steps and I asked, "You sure you got this?"

"We've got this. Besides, Ellie will be here next week and she's worse than Mom. She'll have us scrubbing heads by the third day. Now, get out of here. I'll call if we need you," Morgan said.

Jas stood with her back to the boat with her gear on the dock, looking at something on her phone. I took a deep breath to calm the jitters in my stomach and walked softly up behind her. I dropped my large duffle next to hers and her eyes shot up to mine.

She looked away from me for several long seconds and

my chest tightened fearing I might have misjudged what might happen. She turned back to face me biting her lip and her lower eyelids held a trace of tears that she'd managed fight from spilling over onto her cheeks.

"Lot a gear just to ride with me to the airport."

"Yeah, well, I thought I'd ride along a little further than just the airport," I said.

"How much further?"

I looked down at my bag and back up to meet her eyes. "All the way. Would that be okay with you?"

Jas stepped up close and stretched to kiss me and then whispered, "That's the best idea you've had since we met."

Clapping erupted on the deck as the *Water Horse* peanut gallery whooped and whistled.

"Well it's about dang time!" Rudy shouted giving us a dismissive "get outta here" wave before disappearing back into the cabin hatch with Harper in tow.

Our ride pulled up, and I picked up my duffle. "But I'm not carrying your gear," I said, as I walked toward the taxi. She fast walked past me, bags in hand, and jabbed my sore ribs on her way by.

"Awww, you're really not helping the healing," I moaned.

"We'll see about that, sailor."

Author's Note

In 1945 when Germany surrendered to the Allied forces, their navy had completed construction on nearly one hundred newly designed U-boats. These new subs were so advanced that, at the time, the Allies possessed no practical defense against them. Luckily, only two of the new XXI boats launched for active patrol by the time Germany surrendered. If the Allied naval fleets had been forced to contend with a pack of one hundred of these deadly wolves, it would most likely have changed the face of the war. Besides the increased speed and their ability to carry twenty torpedoes, the XXI's biggest design advantage was its ability to run submerged for long periods of time, making them almost impossible to detect. They accomplished that by adding an advanced snorkel, which provided fresh air to the submarine without surfacing. The XXI U-boats were in fact so advanced that after the war, that aspects of their designs and features were used in US and other country's submarines for the next two decades and beyond. The X-601 however, is a figment of my imagination. If the German Navy could design and build one hundred of the most advanced subs ever conceived at the time, I imagined their engineers might already have the next design in the works.

As a fun behind the story detail, the character Edward Worley of US Naval Intelligence is based on my grandfather Ed Worley. When he was sixteen, his single mother lied about his age on an enlistment form, and before his seventeenth birthday, he waded through the mud with fellow marines in one of the bloodiest campaigns in the Pacific Theater on Guadalcanal. After four years as a marine, he reenlisted in the Navy and served twenty years aboard an aircraft carrier. Although he was never part of Naval Intelligence, he was one of the greatest men I've ever known, and the way he led his life served as a constant reminder that he was part of the greatest generation.

The details of a specific group of neo-Nazi extremists driven by the desire to raise up a Fourth Reich is also fictional . . . I hope. Extremists factions centered around these ideologies have certainly been present across Europe at times. In this time when polarized ideologies seem to drive so much of the dynamics of our society, I hope we look to the past as a lesson for the devastation that extreme division and polarization can leave it its wake. I'd like to think that Michael was on to something when he suggested that although world politics and societies issues aren't simple, maybe at times we're making it a little too complicated. After all, I think most of us would agree we're all just working toward enjoying that metaphorical backyard cookout with the people we love.

Until then, the Water Horse team will search for new assignments filled with action and adventure on the world's waterways. And with every challenge, they'll strive to be examples that "good" is a powerful weapon.

Stay up to date on upcoming Waterway Chronicle Adventures by visiting matthewgorebooks.com. Subscribe and receive a free origin story novella to the Waterway Chronicle series in kindle or audiobook formats, entitled *Clear Waters*.

Until next time, fair winds and safe harbors.

About the Author

MATTHEW GORE is a 30-year-veteran video director and editor and sought after storyteller whose talents transcend both the screen and the page. His work has earned him multiple prestigious awards in the world of television and video production

Self-proclaimed as nautically obsessed, Matthew and his enterprising wife, Darla, moved aboard their beautiful fantail trawler, *Ancient Mariner*, to experience a life tempo unique only to living on the water.

Matthew's love for the sea and adventure shines through in his ocean-based action-adventure "Waterway Chronicle" books. In these gripping tales, readers follow the exploits of Michael and Morgan Gannon, aboard their home, the one-hundred-forty-foot ship *Water Horse*, that serves as the base for Water Horse Expeditions.

With each page, Matthew takes you along with his cast of characters into a world of thrilling escapades and nautical mysteries that unfold against a backdrop of waves, gadgets, and guns on the boundless oceans and waterways of the world. Dive into the excitement and shove off with Matthew on the next Waterway Chronicle Adventure.